PRAISE FOR K. BROMBERG

"K. Bromberg always delivers intelligently written, emotionally intense, sensual romance . . ."

—*USA Today*

"K. Bromberg makes you believe in the power of true love."
—#1 *New York Times* bestselling author Audrey Carlan

"A poignant and hauntingly beautiful story of survival, second chances, and the healing power of love. An absolute must-read."
—*New York Times* bestselling author Helena Hunting

"An irresistibly hot romance that stays with you long after you finish the book."
—#1 *New York Times* bestselling author Jennifer L. Armentrout

"Bromberg is a master at turning up the heat!"
—*New York Times* bestselling author Katy Evans

"Supercharged heat and full of heart. Bromberg aces it from the first page to the last."
—*New York Times* bestselling author Kylie Scott

ALSO BY K. BROMBERG

Published by JKB Publishing, LLC

ISBN: 978-1-942832-41-6

Cover design by Perfect Pear Creative Covers
Cover Image by Wander Aguiar
Cover Model: Brady Ervin
Editing by Marion Making Manuscripts
Formatting by Champagne Book Design
Printed in the United States of America

C—

Happy belated birthday . . . I won't forget next time.

HARD *to* LOVE

Prologue

Finn

16 Years Ago

"Where are you taking me? I'm supposed to pick Molly up in fifteen minutes."

I glance over to my dad and watch the headlights from passing cars reflect off his glasses and face casting it in a mixture of lights and shadows. But he has that expression. The one that tells me he's upset or angry and I dread finding out what I've done wrong this time to irritate him.

Every little thing sets him off these days.

Every. Little. Thing.

"You're not putting enough time in at practice. The only way you're ever going to amount to anything good is by putting the time in. I'm beginning to think you just don't have it in you, son. Year after year, I've told you exactly what you need to do and how you need to do it and—" He tsks followed by a sigh that has me glancing back his way again.

Where are we going?

"But you just don't seem to listen. To hear me. And so, I think it's time I show you exactly what I mean. Precisely the number one lesson you need to learn so that you start thinking straight."

"Dad." I clear my throat. "Sir?"

Why are we in the school parking lot? Why is Molly's car here when I'm supposed to be picking her up in ten minutes?

"You need to learn that women are nothing more than a distraction.

They will play you, win your heart, and then screw you over, leaving you with nothing left just like your mother did to you and me." He grits out the words I've heard more times than I care to count. Ones I discount because even though I'm mad at her for leaving us, she's still my mom. She still loved me somehow. She still . . ."Females are fleeting temptations who distract you from your goals so that by the time they are done with you, you've given up everything."

"What are we doing here?" I all but shout at him, frustrated with this bullshit and desperate to see Molly and hopefully get to second (*or third*) base tonight.

"We are proving a point." My father points at the front of the school gymnasium where Molly is standing beneath the lights. She has one hand toying with the locket on her necklace while she shifts back and forth on her feet, laughing with someone I can't quite see.

Every one of my seventeen years falls a little bit harder for her. The long brown hair, the even longer legs, her tits beneath that tank top, her smile . . . yes, I've got it bad.

Then confusion takes over as Eddie Hamlin, the object of Molly's attention, and the one she's giving that same smile I thought she reserved for me, steps out of the shadows. I don't know why I hold my breath, but I do.

And then I feel like my heart explodes in my chest when she grabs the hem of his shirt—just like she does mine—and pulls him into her until their lips meet. Until they kiss. Until his hands slide up her sides and then rest on her ass so that he can pull her against him.

Just. Like. I. Do.

Molly?

They take a step backward so her back is pressed against the wall.

And Eddie?

Her hands slide around his neck and play with the hair at the nape of his neck just like she does to me.

My girl and *my teammate?*

I don't think.

What the ever-loving-fuck?

I react.

I'm out of the car in a second, barely registering my father's chuckle.

"Molly?" I shout as I jog over to where the two of them stand.

"It's not what you think." Molly jumps back, her expression a picture of guilt and shock.

"*What I think?*" I sputter. "Eddie? What the hell, man?"

Fury and confusion laced with hurt own me as I shove against his chest. He stumbles backward from the force. Other students come out of the gym, the lure of a fight irresistible to them.

But I refuse to be their amusement. Refuse to let my embarrassment be the talk of the school.

My hands are fisted and I curse the tears that burn in my eyes. I blink them away and take a few steps back, unsure what to do, uncertain how this happened.

"I don't understand," I whisper as the crowd grows and tears fill Molly's eyes. She shakes her head.

I want to believe the regret I see on her face is genuine, but this is the same girl who told me she loved me last month. The same girl I loved.

And I believed that to be true so why should I trust myself?

I need to get out of here. I need to breathe. I need to—

Without a word, I turn and jog back to the car where my dad is still sitting behind the wheel.

"Finn," he says way too calmly as I slam the door.

"Drive. Get me out of here," I say, my voice hoarse, those tears back in my eyes.

But he doesn't start the car. Instead, he sits with his hands on the wheel staring at Molly who's now looking our way.

"Now you understand what I've been telling you all these years. Women are nothing but traitors. They use you, then spit you out. You need to learn to use them and spit them out before they dig their hooks in. Once that happens, you'll feel like you do right now. Hurt. Raw. Angry. Just like your mom made me feel. And you, Finn. Because of what she did *to us.*"

"Not now, Dad." But his words hit my ears differently this time. They start to hold some truth. They start to feel valid.

"Women always leave. Remember that."

He finally turns the key in the ignition and slowly pulls out of the spot and away from my bullseye view of Molly and Eddie. *Thank God.* I hate them. I hate them both. But how did my dad know to bring me here?

How did he know they'd be standing right there and what we'd find?

And why did he laugh as my heart was ripped from my chest and stomped on?

Chapter ONE

Finn

I HOP ON ONE FOOT IN THE DARK AS I TRY TO PUT MY SHOE ON without tripping over the piles of shit on the floor throughout the room.

Too late.

I lose my balance and smack my thigh against the corner of her dresser.

Motherfucker. I grab my leg, my shoe still half on, and grit my teeth in response to the pain as I stare through the darkness toward the bed.

"Finn?" Roxy's sleep-drugged voice calls.

I freeze with my hand on the zipper of my slacks. *Shit. So much for making a clean getaway.*

"Where are you going?" she asks as she shifts in bed so that she's sitting there, a shadow against the night.

I hesitate for the briefest of seconds, thoughts of her warm body and her more than wild ways filling my head. But right after those thoughts are her words from earlier tonight.

"We're good together, you and me. Maybe I shouldn't renew my lease and we could . . . you know, move in together." And if that wasn't enough to make my dick wither and fall off, there was the soft sigh of "I love you, Finn," that she whispered when she thought I had fallen asleep. The four words nearly stopped my heart.

Jesus. It took everything I had to not leave right then and there.

Live together? Surrounded by all this clutter? By not having the freedom to come and go as I please?

Love? Let's face it. She doesn't know the first thing about love and neither do I. No, it's time to stop while I'm ahead.

And while I'm in control of the situation.

Time to go.

"Finn?"

"Clients. I have clients," I mutter as I step and trip over one of her numerous piles of clothes on the floor.

Note to self: stay away from the boho-chic chicks. They have too much shit everywhere.

Oh, but then there are the Kama Sutra positions they love . . .

"Clients? It's two in the morning. What do you mean clients?"

Fuck. It is two.

"I just got a text. He got himself into trouble. I need to deal with him."

For the love of God, just get me out of here.

"Come back to bed," she says, and I can hear her pat the mattress as if that will convince me.

"No. I got a text." I slip on my other shoe and successfully avoid any other run-ins with the corner of a piece of furniture. "A client got in an altercation and needs my help."

"I thought you were an agent. Not a lawyer."

"I'm their . . . everything." *But I'm not yours.* I push the button on my phone so the screen lights up in the dark and it looks like I'm getting a text. "See? That's him again."

She huffs loudly before flopping back on the bed—a sound that feels victorious for me so long as I don't trip on another pile of her crap before I get out the front door. "So, see you tonight?" she asks, hope tingeing the edges of her tone.

"Um, I can't. I have to catch a flight to Michigan," I make up on the fly.

"Michigan?"

Michigan? Where the hell did that come from?

"Yeah. I don't know when I'll be back." I stop at the door and look back at her for effect. I know she's looking—chicks always do—and the last thing I want to do is be a dick when I'm dumping her. I mean, she doesn't know it, but I am.

"Okay, then. Call me when you get back?"

"Of course."

And with that, I bolt for the front door as I slip my hand into the arm of my dress shirt, desperate to be out of this patchouli-smelling, crystal-filled apartment on the Lower West Side.

I wait until I'm out of the building and away from her to breathe a sigh of relief.

Glad to have that distraction over with.

Or at least until I have to dodge her phone calls and texts that no doubt will be coming in a few days.

Chapter TWO

Stevie

THE MUSIC IS LOUD ON THE POOL DECK BEFORE ME. ONE HUNDRED or so people in bathing suits dance on the small stage with their hands up and alcohol sloshing over the sides of their glasses onto those around them.

But nobody cares.

They're here in Las Vegas to party.

To let loose.

Doing exactly what I should be doing right now.

I hold my hand to my forehead and glare at Carson from behind my darkened sunglasses where I lie on a chaise lounge. What number lecture of the day is this? Eighth? Ninth? And it's just after one o'clock in the afternoon.

"You're killing my buzz, Carson," I mutter as I try to look around where he stands to see what the crowd is cheering over now. But he shifts so I'm forced to look at him and his formal dress shirt rolled up at the sleeves and slacks with pleats in the front that have no business here at the poolside party club at The Venetian. My killjoy of a manager.

"Then maybe you shouldn't be buzzed at this hour. In fact, maybe you should be figuring out how best to explain the images splashed all over social media from last night."

"God forbid precious Stevie Lancaster lets loose a little," I say, sarcasm lacing every syllable as I rest my head back on the lounger and close my eyes.

"Better yet, maybe you should be out on the court with Kellen, getting your reps in. Your backhand needs work before the next Open."

"Go away, Carson." I pick up my cell and start thumbing through it, not really paying any attention to what I'm seeing, but more just trying to prove the point that I'm not paying attention to him.

The last thing I need to do is be on the court with Kellen where he says things my dad would tell me but that sound so very different. So much so that I immediately tense up and shank the ball.

"He told me you didn't show up to yesterday's training, and by the look of the empty glasses on the table beside you, it doesn't seem that you'll be showing up today either."

I shrug dramatically to reinforce how bored I am with him. With his babysitting. Anything to make the fun police go away.

"I'm taking a break, Carson. Is that not allowed?" I ask, knowing damn well that under the reign of Liam Lancaster, breaks—*hell, fun*—were never allowed. All work. No play. All hustle. Every moment of every day. "I've been reading up on sports training theories," I lie. "The article I read this morning, and that I've decided will be my motto for today said it was good for the elite athlete's mind, soul, and body to have a few days off to cut loose every now and again. It reinvigorates the athlete and re-adjusts their mindset." The smile I give him is sugary sweet and dripping with insincerity.

"So that's what you call dancing on bar tops, taking over the stripper pole at Sapphire's—"

"It was a dare, *and* I had my clothes on." I sigh, trying to remember through the haze of last night's alcohol. "You should really try the Cards O' Fun. It's clear you need some added spontaneity in your life."

"*Cards O' Fun?*" he asks.

"Yep. Vivi and Jordan made them up," I say referring to my two oldest friends from the tennis circuit we played in as kids. While they long ago gave up the competitive end of the game, our friendship has endured. And perhaps they have been the source of more than one lecture between Carson and me, so I'm bringing them up just to piss him off. "Every night

I have to pick two cards from the deck they've created and complete the tasks."

"Tasks such as pole-dancing and what else?"

"You've seen the social media posts. You can guess."

"Couldn't you guys have opted for a game of Monopoly or Yahtzee?" He chuckles.

"Now that wouldn't be very adventurous, would it?"

He stares at me and I can't figure out what he is thinking. "So you pull two cards and have to complete the tasks or else what?"

I shrug flippantly. "Have you ever known me to lose at anything? They may be my girls, but I will not be the first to chicken out."

"This isn't a joke, Stevie."

"Clearly, considering you're always so damn serious," I say mocking his tone.

"I know you're struggling with your father's death and—"

"You don't have a clue what I'm—"

"But it's like you're trying to throw away everything you've worked for. Everything he helped and guided you to be. You were in peak condition and now it's as if you're purposefully poisoning your body with all this crap so you have an excuse when you fail." He takes a step closer so that his shadow covers my face, just in case my eyes were closed because the sun was too much when looking at him.

Nope. Not the reason.

More like I don't want to be lectured.

"I turned pro at age fifteen and have been going nonstop for almost ten years, Car. I've worked—"

"Exactly, and since your dad passed, you've acted like life's one never-ending party."

Another roar goes up from the party crowd and it's the distraction I need to shove his words away and pretend I didn't hear him.

Like I needed to be reminded that he's dead.

Because it's not as if every time I step on the court, I don't hear his voice and turn to look for him to be reminded he's not there. Or every knock on my hotel room door doesn't have my heart lurching into my throat, expecting him to be mad I'm running late for my conditioning.

Every second of every day I'm reminded. He may have been a tyrant but he was also my anchor, and now, I feel like I'm adrift at sea. That is *not* struggling with my father's death. *That's called drowning in it.*

I lift a drink from the table beside me and suck on the straw until slurping sounds let me know I've hit the bottom of the glass. I suck one more time to make the sound on purpose.

Shit. I need another and I definitely can't with Killjoy Carson standing with his hands on his hips and his judgment front and center.

"Can you at least move to the left, Car? There's a hot guy over there who you're blocking, and I want a direct line of sight."

"Christ," he mutters but shifts out of the way to earn the smirk I give him. His sigh weighs down the lighthearted atmosphere I'm trying to enjoy. "You've left me no choice, kid."

I'm not your kid.

But I don't respond. I don't even acknowledge that he's spoken. It's so much easier to fixate on all the people partying, feeling good, living a life I don't understand but have been trying to lose myself in for a while.

"You will be in my suite tomorrow morning at ten a.m. prompt."

I don't respond.

"Stevie." My name is a frustrated, patriarchal sigh.

"*Ten?*" I groan despite a part of me feeling surprised at this demanding side of Carson. "That's so early when the girls and I have Cards O' Fun to finish tonight." I sigh heavily and look at my nails as if I'm checking my manicure.

"Failure to do so will result in me pulling you out of the US Open and losing two major sponsors. You're in no way prepared, and I refuse to allow you to show up and make an ass out of yourself."

The US Open. My dad's favorite tournament. The place where, as a little girl, I sat on his knee, listening as he told me how it would be when I stepped foot on the court someday.

And then the next day, he'd take me on our practice court and run drills until I thought my arms and legs would fall off.

I don't let a single emotion flicker over my face, although I feel like every single one runs through me.

"I'm not prepared?" I snort. "I have two and a half months. Get over yourself and your power trip."

His smile reveals a flicker of disdain. "If my promises to your father meant nothing to me then I'd let you stay on this path you're on. I might even take pleasure when you fall on your ass in front of the world while on center court. But those promises meant something to me, Stevie. They truly did."

I avert my eyes and try to blink away the tears that threaten. It would be easier if I fired Carson. If I told him he was an old man who didn't understand me or how things worked now, but I'd be lying. I'd know deep down that my dad would have picked him because he knew his shit and would protect me.

And maybe I resent Carson for that. That he knew about my dad being sick when I didn't.

"Stevie?" he asks, impatience weighing down his voice.

"I'll see what I can do about it. You can't expect a girl to change her plans on such short notice."

His chuckle holds anything but amusement in it.

Maybe I've pushed him too far. Maybe I haven't.

Question is, how much do I care? I bite my bottom lip and stare past him and his well-meaning pep talk to let him know he's dismissed.

"Have your last bit of fun tonight. Get drunk, fuck who you want, toy with who you don't, get whatever the hell you need to out of your system—"

"Wow, such language. Anyone listening would think you're mad at me or something." I bat my eyelashes, even though he can't see them behind my darkened shades.

He takes another step toward me, leans over, and lowers his voice when he speaks. "Have your last night of *Cards O' Fun*, Lancaster, but try to be discreet, will you? There's already way too much press, too much damage to your image, and I'm the one who has to try and repair it."

"No one gave you that job," I say like the petulant child I know I'm being.

"Your father did." The words hang in the air like lead. "He entrusted it to me and you damn well better know that I plan on keeping my promise to him."

My stomach twists in knots and my heart races at the mere mention of him. "Great. My condolences on having the job no one wants." I motion for him to get out of the way but he doesn't move. "If you're going to stand there, you could at least be useful and get me another drink or two."

"Ten o'clock, Stevie."

"Yeah, yeah," I mutter, giving him a salute before motioning to the waitress circling the VIP section for another drink without so much as a look Carson's way.

He clears his throat, the weight of his stare pinning me motionless. "He'd be disappointed in this. *In you.*"

Each word feels like a battering ram to my solar plexus. A direct hit of guilt and pain and hurt.

The problem is, those are the things fueling me, driving me, pushing me to act this way.

Carson meant to correct me with those words and he has no clue he just poured gasoline on a smoldering fire. Because my dad—my purpose, the only one I ever tried to please—is gone.

And nothing—not winning, partying, practicing, nor trying—will ever bring him back.

Chapter THREE

Stevie

"I NEED SOME EXCITEMENT," I SAY AS I SET DOWN MY EMPTY DRINK on the space next to the vacant slot machine.

Tick. Tick. Tick.

The clock is ticking on my freedom.

I'm not naïve to what Carson has in mind for me. Some prissy PR executive to stalk in tomorrow morning—maybe it's today because I have no idea what time it is—in her high heels and too-perfect hair and tell me exactly how we need to reimagine and repackage my image.

Tick. Tick. Tick.

Back to pristine white tennis skirts and walking the fucking tightrope I've lived all twenty-four of my years on so far.

Tick. Tick. Tick.

"It's my last night of freedom for a while," I groan to Vivi, my number one enabler who is standing beside me surveying the lay of the land. She and Jordan flew out here five days ago at my request, knowing that without my dad, I've felt so untethered. *Alone.*

And since then, we've been living our best life. Something that is completely outside the norm for me and my typical seven-day training, clean-eating, and no-alcohol regime.

"And?" Jordan says, a mischievous smile sliding on her red-painted lips. "If it's your last night of freedom, then I guess we better get moving." Her laugh rings out above the electronic noises of the machines surrounding us.

"You've got your wig on," Vivi says as she motions to my dark brown wig that shocked the shit out of me when I saw my reflection in the mirror. It was so real looking I did a double take—me, but so very different looking. "So you're covered from the media catching wind of any trouble we willingly get in."

My grin widens. The feeling of freedom is still so new and liberating that it's like a high for me. "The question is, what trouble might that be?" I laugh and then close my eyes for a beat, allowing the alcohol blitz to make the room spin a bit before meeting the expectant gazes of my closest friends.

"We've danced. We've drank," Jordan says. "We've flirted our asses off and kissed our share of hot men—"

"Jordan and I have completed our two Cards O' Fun for the night. You've only done one so far," Vivi says as she holds up the last sealed envelope by her two fingers, a more than coy smile on her lips. "It's time for you to pick your last one, Stevie . . . unless of course, you're not brave enough to do it?"

"Why do I get the feeling that I'm not going to like this?" I say as I look from Vivi to Jordan and then back again.

"Are you accusing *moi* of rigging Cards O' Fun?" Vivi asks in a way that makes me know she definitely has.

"Give it to me," I say, snatching the envelope from her hand and tearing it open to find out what awaits me. I unfold the piece of paper inside and read the words written there: *have a one-night stand.*

I stare at the dare on the piece of paper and don't say a word as I try to process it. Not so much process it but rather consider how I get the nerve up to do it since I don't exactly have ample experience like they do.

Being a wild child is one thing—*that* I can handle. Sleeping with some random stranger is a different realm for me.

But I can't deny the hum that's just beneath the surface from the idea. The thrill of doing something that is normal and typical of anyone my age.

Jordan nudges me. "If you're hell-bent on sowing your wild oats,

Stevie, then the number one way to own that is to have a reckless one-night stand."

"And you conveniently planned for *this card* to be pulled on my last night of freedom, didn't you?"

Vivi's shrug is less than apologetic. Her smile even more so. "C'mon, girlfriend. You've missed out on so many normal things in life that the rest of us have *lived*. All we want is for you to have *lived a little* too."

Wasn't that what I'd griped at them about a few weeks ago? That I felt so young compared to them. That despite having traveled the world many times over and experienced things that most people would kill for, I still have missed out on so many rites of passage.

"C'mon, Steves," Jordan says in her sweetest voice. "You know the idea is exciting. A hot guy. Unapologetic sex. No strings attached. And after, you simply walk away. Besides, with this get-up," she says tugging on my dark brown wig, "no one will know it's you."

I stare at her, my bravado uncertain about what side it wants to stand on—in or out. I can count on two hands the number of men/boys I've kissed. I can count on less than one hand the number of men I've slept with.

It's always been about tennis. Always been my father stepping in when things got too serious to point out whoever I was with was not good enough or that he was with me for the wrong reasons.

Handcuffed.

My personal life has been like this for so long. Controlled. Managed.

Does the idea make me nervous as hell? Of course, it does. And yet I've heard stories from Vivi and Jordan about how exhilarating it is. How rebellious and thrilling it is to sleep with someone when you might not even know their real name.

"So . . ." Vivi asks.

. . . unless of course, you're not brave enough to do it . . .

"Fine. Yes. I'll do it." My shaky inhale doesn't reflect the resolve my words are spoken with, but I nod to emphasize it. It doesn't matter though, because it's drowned out by their squeals that are a mixture of both excitement and victory.

"Now it's time you pick some unsuspecting man *to fuck*," Vivi completes for her.

"Vivi!" I shriek and bat at her arm as a lascivious smile slides on my lips, and my body suddenly hums for a release I didn't realize I needed.

"What?" She shrugs unabashedly. "We *are* in the City of Sin so get ready to sin. You look hot and like a woman about to do something she's never done before. Besides, you'll have something to reminisce about while you're back in your own personal hell doing drill after drill after drill on the court."

"She has a point," Jordan adds.

"If this is truly your last night of fun before *Killjoy Carson* takes hold like you think, then we think you need to go out with a bang."

"Literally." Jordan laughs and then stands on her tiptoes as she begins scouring the floor around us.

"It's the last card." Vivi plucks the card from my hands. "And we agreed we'd accomplish every last item before No Fun Carson steals you back from us."

Fear snakes up my spine. The sex part is fine. It's the *some random guy* part that stresses me out.

"You're thinking too much," Jordan says.

"But—"

"There are no buts unless the one we're talking about is the one you'll be tapping tonight." Vivi taps her fingernails against her glass. "Now the question is, *whose will it be?*"

"We need someone a bit older. A man who's old enough to know what he's doing but not so old that he can't get it up," Jordan says.

"Jesus." I choke on the drink the cocktail waitress just handed me.

"She's right though," Jordan says and then grunts and stills when she sees someone across the way. "You only get tonight so we need to make sure he's worth the time. What about him?"

We all look toward the blackjack pit where a man is buttoning up his suit jacket. He's tall with dark skin, a killer smile, and an air about him that screams swagger and sex appeal.

Can't say I'd mind that.

But my hopes are dashed before they can really get started when a woman walks up and plants a kiss on his lips.

We all groan and then start our search anew. Mr. One-night Only has to be here somewhere. No complications. Great sex. I mean, I can hope that's the case—for my sake at least.

Although, I guess that's not necessarily required to finish the game.

Chapter FOUR

Stevie

IT'S SLOW GOING, BUT WE MAKE UP FOR IT BY DRINKING MORE ALCOHOL and moving locations. A nightclub. Another bar. Jumping on the go-go dancers' platforms and dancing there until we were asked to leave.

The night wears thin, the alcohol buzzes through our veins, and the prospects for my very picky self, seem even thinner.

Normally I'd be thrilled to have an out on this dare . . . but if it means losing to them, not a chance in hell.

"You'd think of all the cities in the world that this would be the one where we'd have the best luck, but . . ." Vivi's words fade off and then her low, rich hum is a taunt all in itself, begging us to turn and look to where her attention is focused.

Yes.

That's the first thought that comes to mind when I lay my eyes on the man who just entered the bar area.

He's tall with dark hair and broad shoulders. He wears an expensive dress shirt that's unbuttoned at the collar with his shirtsleeves rolled up to showcase taut forearms and what looks to be a Rolex.

He's a man who knows he looks good and owns it. A man who commands attention when he walks into a room and he definitely has mine.

"*Hello, gorgeous,*" Jordan murmurs around her straw.

He nonchalantly surveys the room as if he's looking to see if there's anyone worthy of his time.

Apparently, I am because when he looks in our direction, his eyes find and then remain on mine. I don't flinch, don't look away. My expression doesn't even reflect the thrill that shoots through me because the man who caught my eye might be interested in me as well.

Our gazes hold. His eyes narrow as he unabashedly takes me in, assesses, approves. Then when I assume he likes what he sees, a ghost of a smile—arrogance and sex appeal, a man who knows he's good-looking—is offered.

It's embarrassing that his smirk alone has me wanting him.

Embarrassing but it's true.

"Your move, Stevie," Vivi murmurs.

My move.

With a deep breath, I push away from the bar and stride across the room—maybe with a little extra swing to my hips—to approach him.

I'm too buzzed to give the ramifications of my actions too much thought. Too lost in the challenge, and reclaiming some of my independence, to think of all the things my dad had drilled into my head that would have scared me off doing something like this before. The *what if* he's crazy? The *what if* he's a plant to get an exclusive on me? The *what if* he's a serial killer?

But isn't that why I'm here? Why I'm even doing this—*besides of course what I like about him*—to block out everything that's just too much. Responsibility. Duty. Grief. *Simply being Stevie Lancaster and all the trappings that come with her.*

"Hi," I breathe, unable to take my eyes off him. He's even more gorgeous up close.

"Hello yourself," he murmurs as he leans an elbow against a table and makes no qualms about taking everything about me in. His hazel eyes framed by thick lashes run the length of my body and when they come back up to meet my eyes, that effortless smile is an aphrodisiac all itself.

"I'm Scarlett," I say and hold a hand out to him, refusing to break his stare.

"Scarlett whose name isn't really Scarlett," he says and shakes my hand. "It's a most unexpected pleasure to meet you. *I'm Rhett.*"

"Rhett, huh?" My lips quirk into a smile. A man who knows classic movies *and* knows how to play this game. Unexpected but more than welcome. My hand remains in his longer than it should, and I can't say that I mind. "Nice to meet you too."

"Would you like a drink?" he asks placing his hand on the small of my back and leading me to the bar before I can respond.

"Sure. Yes." *What in the hell am I doing?* I take the seat he offers and welcome the chance to talk rather than head straight upstairs. Especially when Vivi and Jordan are standing in view just over his shoulder where I can see them watching us while silently giving me fist pumps. "What'll you have?" I ask.

"I believe that's my question considering I asked you if you'd like a drink," he says with a ghost of a smile.

We stare at each other for a beat, a small battle of wills over who's in control, before I clear my throat and let him know what to order for me. It's a small concession in the scheme of things.

He places our drink orders, his attention on the bartender, while mine is fully on him. "What exactly are we doing?"

Brilliant question, Stevie. Freaking brilliant. It takes everything I have not to roll my eyes.

"It seems self-explanatory. A drink or two. A little conversation. Perhaps some flirting."

"Flirting?" I ask as he shifts in his seat, and I get the hint of a sculpted chest from beneath his open dress shirt.

"Yes. I'm more than certain a woman as gorgeous as yourself knows exactly how to do that," he says as he slides money across the bar and hands me my drink.

"I'm sure I do." There's a moment where we stare at each other as if we're the only two people in this bar. And it's weird for me, not the being attracted to him part, but rather my almost desperate want for him to like me—when normally I couldn't care less.

"So, *Scarlett*," he says, "I take it you're not from Vegas?"

"No. Just visiting."

"And you decided that of all the men in the bar, I'm the one you want to target." There is an aloofness in his tone. An incredulity to it that tells me he might not be game for my sudden interest.

I'm not sure how that makes me feel.

"Why am I getting the feeling that you find my interest in you hard to believe?" I ask as I play with the straw in my drink. "Should I be worried that I've picked the wrong man to set my sights on?"

He chuckles. "That remains to be seen . . . but I'm just curious as to *why.*"

"Why?" I ask.

"Yes. *Why?*" He glances over his shoulder and waves to where Vivi and Jordan are pretending miserably not to be monitoring what the two of us are doing. "How do I know this isn't some game that you and your friends have concocted to see who could get a guy to bite first for some ridiculous prize? Or better yet, how do I know this isn't some scam where you're going to take me up to my hotel room, tie me up, and then the three of you are going to rob me blind?"

I stare at him, at his coy smile and playful eyes, and secretly love that he's not a pushover. Too many men are when it comes to a beautiful woman and even the remote chance of getting lucky with her. *Not that I know from personal experience or anything.*

"Tying you up? That remains to be seen," I say, repeating his words back to him and hoping the words come off as sexy when they feel so lame on my lips. "But one thing's for sure, this isn't a game, and I'm not a con artist."

"Then what is it?" he asks as he swings my barstool so that both of my knees are between his, placing a hand on my bare leg.

My heart lurches at the connection, and I pray he doesn't feel my pulse pounding beneath his touch.

"It's me looking across the bar and finding you compelling and attractive. It's me having one more night before I have to return to the everyday grind of my life and wanting to live a little." I lean in close to him so he can smell my perfume and feel the heat of my breath against his ear when I whisper, "It's me wanting to feel a little. Trust me when I say that's all it is."

"Trust is a tricky thing," he murmurs as his fingers close around my wrist and hold it still. I meet him stare for stare and don't back down until he murmurs, "*Jesus*," and the rumble of that word has anticipation fluttering in my stomach.

"What about you? Should I guess? You're here in Vegas for work. You're some kind of high-power someone who enjoys being in control and telling people exactly what they should and shouldn't be doing. While you're not opposed to the temptations of the casino, it's really not your thing considering your need for control, so what you really want is someone to hook up with. Someone who has no objections to a quick one-night stand where the woman you sleep with doesn't tell you her real name nor promise to whisper sweet nothings in your ear. And after said fun, she walks out while you head to your meetings tomorrow no worse for the wear."

"That's quite a supposition," he says, head angling to the side, and all traces of his playful smile are gone as he studies me.

"It is, but then again, it's true, isn't it?"

"Perhaps, but there is such a thing as coming on too strong." He leans in close and whispers, "Anything worth wanting should be slightly harder to get."

His words hit me in a way that's foreign to me. Rejection isn't something I'm used to, and I do believe he just rejected me.

"And yet you're intrigued." I run my tongue over my bottom lip to lick away a drop of my drink. He notices. He definitely notices. "*Interested even.*"

"Who said I was interested?" he asks as he shifts his gaze and then his head to eye a woman who walks past us.

I clear my throat. "Eyes on the prize, Rhett."

"Old habits die hard, sweetheart." He laughs and shakes his glass so the ice clinks against its sides. "Where were we again?"

My laugh is low and taunting, my bravado definitely back in place. The fingernail I draw up the center of his chest even more so as I entice him to only have eyes for me. "You're interested all right. You can sit here and act like right now your cock isn't begging you to say yes, but it is. Your mind's still processing but your body is already in the elevator heading upstairs."

Oh my God. Did I really just say that? Did those words actually come out of my mouth?

Yes. Yes, they did.

He lifts an eyebrow as a chuckle falls from between his sexy lips. "What if I said no?"

"Then you'd be a fool to pass this up," I state matter-of-factly.

"Think quite highly of yourself, don't you?"

I shrug unapologetically. "Lucky for you I do because you're the only one who's walked in here tonight that has had me looking twice."

"I'm not sure if that's a compliment or an insult." He shifts in his chair so that his inner thighs rub against my outer ones. I refuse to admit to myself that the sudden hitch in my breath is in reaction to his touch.

"Does any of that really matter if, after the next few drinks, I'm going to ask you to take me up to your room?"

He gives a shake of his head and smirks as his eyes hold mine in a way that unnerves and turns me on all at once. And without pretext or preamble, Rhett slides a hand to the back of my neck and brings his mouth to mine.

He doesn't coax my lips open with his tongue, but rather assumes I'll open for him. He doesn't ask, he just takes. With his lips and his tongue and the scrape of his stubble against my chin and with the dominant slide of his hand from my neck to my cheek.

He tastes of the whiskey he's drinking and of desire that matches what's thrumming through my veins. He's not hurried in his kiss. It's slow but demanding, soft but wanting, and has every nerve in my body standing at attention as I lift my hands and fist them around his biceps.

Now this? This is a kiss most definitely worth waiting for.

The sounds of the slot machines fade away. The chatter of those around us disappears. His kiss owns me in the best ways possible and hints (hopefully) at the thoroughness of other things he does just as well.

And before I can process that it's over, Rhett breaks his lips from mine. Without a word, he sits back with a satisfied, smug smile curling up the corners of that tempting mouth of his.

I'm sitting here before him acting like I'm unaffected when in reality,

I feel like I was just thoroughly knocked on my ass. A part of me hates that he doesn't look how I feel—wanting more when I'm not a woman who gets weak in the knees.

But my knees are weak and the apex of my thighs ache with want.

Another round of drinks is slid before us but neither of us breaks from looking at one another to notice.

"You'll do," I finally murmur, assuming the words will challenge him to prove he can do better. That he'll drop this game and show me just how much better he can do. And simply because my thoughts fell out of my mouth because I'm too flustered by his kiss to stop them.

"*I'll do?*" He laughs.

"Yep. You passed." I lean back in my seat, adjusting my one leg crossed over my other and subsequently rubbing it ever so slightly along the inseam of his pants.

His body stills, and I can assume his own instincts understand clearly that this is in fact a game I'm playing. Not one with Vivi and Jordan, but one between him and me. Who will cave first? Who will admit they want the other enough to make the first move out of this crowded casino?

"I wasn't aware I was taking a test."

I quirk an eyebrow. "Everything is a test, is it not? Besides, if a man can kiss like that, then there's a supposition he has *other skills* that are just as impressive too."

I make the comment to get a reaction from him but he just sits there swirling his glass and watching the whiskey eddy around its insides. He purses his lips for a beat before his eyes lift to mine. "Do you really want this, *Scarlett?*"

His words have me faltering. "Excuse me?"

"Don't be offended. You're talking with such confidence but there's a waver just beneath it—a flash of uncertainty—that tells me you're not one hundred percent comfortable with what you're trying to pull here."

I despise that he sees through me this easily. That he sees the doubt and uncertainty that hums just beneath the desire. That he realizes as much as I'm trying to be this person, she's not me, but rather I'm just trying on her shoes for the night. Just trying to step outside of the person I'm caged into being and live more than I've been allowed to.

And hell, if a well-deserved orgasm comes with the new shoes I'm trying on, then who am I to say no?

Everybody deserves to live a little outside of their comfort zone, so why is he challenging me while I'm trying to break outside of mine?

"It shouldn't be this hard to get laid," I mutter.

"Ah, but it should if it's worth it." He stands and throws some cash on the bar, as I stare at him with confused shock when he begins to walk away.

"Wait. *What?*" I sputter as his chuckle trails back to me before he turns.

"Are you coming?"

There's a lift of his eyebrow that taunts and says those three words were chosen carefully.

Chapter
FIVE

Stevie

THE NERVES HIT.

As they should for any normal person when she's standing toward the back of an elevator, riding up to floor thirty-four with a man who can kiss her senseless and whose hand feels like it's burning a hole into the small of her back where it rests.

He smiles and nods to passengers who are coming on and off the car while I stand there suddenly freaked out over how I let Vivi and Jordan talk me into this, and at the same time, feeling a rush of adrenaline.

Or is that the alcohol?

Regardless, we're stepping off the elevator and Rhett is escorting me to his room without saying anything. There's only the heat of his body behind me and the crackle of undeniable sexual tension between us.

I can understand it now. What Jordan and Vivi were talking about. *The allure. The excitement. The . . . unknown.*

He slides the key card into the lock. Once the lock clicks to green, he opens and shuts the door, escorting me into a room that's decent but nowhere near what my penthouse looks like. There is paperwork and a laptop on the table near the window that gives a perfect view of the blinking lights on the strip and a suitcase standing unopened on the floor.

We walk a few feet into the room before he turns to me. There's challenge in the look he gives me, almost as if he's saying, "You got what you wanted, now what are you going to do about it?"

My heart is racing and my breath is coming fast. I know I could chicken out, walk out of the room, and just lie to Vivi and Jordan about it to save face . . . but I don't want to. There's nothing wrong with being more than attracted to a man and wanting to enjoy him in every possible way.

With a slow and steady deep breath, I step into Rhett and initiate the first kiss. I slide my hands up the plane of his chest, the crisp dress shirt cool beneath my palms, before sliding them around his neck and slanting my lips over his.

And so the kiss begins. It's a slow dance of lips and tongue, of moans and contented sighs, of my body meeting his as he's pressed against the wall, while his hands still at his sides. Whereas the first kiss downstairs was more of a challenge to test me, this one holds more restraint. It's still erotic and sexy as hell the way his tongue dances with mine and how soft yet demanding his lips are, but he's holding back.

He's not touching me.

His hands are at his sides almost as if he's letting me take the reins when it's *him* I want guiding this, *him* I want controlling this.

I take a step back and break from the kiss. Our eyes meet and a small thrill shoots through me as I take in his lust-heavy eyelids and the impressive bulge pressing against the seam of his pants. His shoulders are rising up and down like mine are as we both try to catch our breath and process the turn this night has taken.

"This isn't a game, Rhett," I murmur as I reach out skim my fingernails over the fabric of his shirt. He watches me, the warmth of his breath hitting my skin, the shift of his gaze to my lips and then back up, sexy as hell. And that in and of itself, spurs me on. "I'm just a confident woman who finds you attractive." I undo the first button. "Who wants you." Another one is undone and it gives me a glimpse of a toned, tanned chest. Nerves give way to desire. "Who wants you to touch her."

And there is something about those six words that are like striking a match. Because with them, Rhett has our position flipped in a heartbeat—me with my back against the wall and him with his body pressing me into it.

His hands move now.

They move in sync with his mouth on mine and then as if it's not enough, he inches up my skirt, his firm fingertips against the softness of my thighs. He slides his hand beneath the lace of my panties and cups my bare ass as he grinds into the V of my thighs.

It's a taunt. A tease. A temptation I want to give in to.

His mouth closes over my breast through the fabric of my tank top and I arch my back, pushing myself into him. The warm heat of his mouth is a sensation all in itself, but it's his fingers finding purchase between my thighs that draws a low moan from me.

He matches my moan with a guttural groan of his own when he slips his fingers beneath my panties to find me warm, wet, and more than willing. I spread my feet farther apart to give him access to take control, as I welcome the onslaught of sensations.

Anything to make me feel something again.

Anything to make me forget everything for just a bit.

My hands go to him. In a flurry of motion, I unbutton the rest of his shirt and with his mouth back on mine, he pulls his arms out of his sleeves. His biceps are firm and the only thing I can grab on to while his fingers are eliciting sensations and pleasure. All I can think about is touching him, feeling him, causing him to make the same strangled moans that are falling from my mouth.

My hands are on his pants. His button. His zipper. Sliding beneath the waistband of his underwear until my fingers wrap around the velvety smooth hardness of him. His groan fills my ears and it's everything I need to hear—he wants this as bad as I do.

He cups me, fingers moving in, the palm of his hand adding pressure to the hub of nerves begging to find its release, all while his lips create a devastating trail of open-mouthed kisses down the curve of my neck, to the shell of my ear, to my collarbone and below.

My body thrums with anticipation and arousal and all I can think is *more*. I want more of him. I need more of him.

Our mouths connect again as his fingers work at a fever pitch to bring me to that cusp of wanting more and begging him to stop until he's in me.

But I'm already past the point of no return. Already tensing my hands on his biceps, already bucking my hips against his hand, already moaning incoherently as the orgasmic haze washes over me.

"Christ," he murmurs, our breaths panting against each other's before his teeth tug gently on my bottom lip. His pants and belt give a clink as they drop around his ankles. "Condom. We need—"

"Yes. Condom. Yes," I say, still dazed by him, by this, by the climax that tore through me without mercy. My lips meet his and my hand runs up and down the length of his shaft one last time.

"Be right back." He steps out of his pants and strides naked into the bathroom giving me a more than ample view of his gorgeous backside and broad shoulders.

But . . . *Oh my God.* My head is spinning as I slide my skirt down to my feet. I feel weak. *Sated.* Dizzy. *I had no freaking idea orgasms could do . . .* that.

Chapter SIX

Finn

CHRIST.

How did this happen?

Not that I'm complaining but a quick trip down to the bar for a drink or two to relax after a long flight was not supposed to end up with a gorgeous woman in my room, and her arousal still wet on my hands while I run to my bathroom to grab a condom to jacket up.

Yet here we are.

I chuckle at the thought as I roll the condom over my cock and stride back into the room.

"All set . . ." But my words fall on deaf ears as I take in the woman, *Scarlett*, who is lying across my bed, wearing high heels, a barely-there lacey bra and panty set that effectively means she's nude.

And she's completely passed out.

"No. No. No," I mutter as I move toward her, dick hardening at the sight of her incredible body, and begin shaking her shoulder to wake her up.

To continue what we started.

But she doesn't budge. Doesn't even stir. And I'm left standing with a rock-hard cock, a blissfully gorgeous woman in my bed, and no relief in sight.

Was she *that* drunk? How did I not realize that?

And more importantly, what the fuck am I supposed to do now?

Clearly I was hoping to have a fun time with her, or I wouldn't have invited her up to my room. But now? Now, she needs to go if sex isn't on the menu.

"Come on, Scarlett. Time to get up. To go home."

One-night stands don't get to sleep in my bed. We have sex. One of us leaves. I shower and rid myself of everything but the memory of her.

End of story.

Then again, most women don't get to sleep in my bed, one-night stand or not, so that's neither here nor there.

But this . . . *her* . . . how do I handle this? It's not like I can pick her up and set her gently in the hallway where she can wake up on her own time.

I'm not that much of a dick.

Is this Karma for boho chic chick? For leaving in the middle of the night and then ignoring her texts and calls?

"Fuck," I groan when I'd rather be groaning for other reasons. I cross my arms over my chest and study the woman in my bed. To say she's gorgeous is an understatement. She has long, brown hair—which I can assume isn't natural since the carpet definitely doesn't match the drapes—pouty, sensual lips, and a body that screams that she puts time in at the gym. She's toned and tanned and hell if I wouldn't have enjoyed my hands being all over her for the next hour or two.

But now I'm here and she's there. "You're being a creep," I mutter to myself. How weird it is to be staring at a passed-out woman while thinking how much I'd have liked to fuck her.

Lucky for her, I'm who she set her sights on tonight and not some other guy who might take advantage of the situation.

I like my women willing, feisty—not comatose.

"C'mon, Scarlett," I say, trying to shake and wake her again to no avail. I walk from one side of the hotel room to the other, weighing my options. Do I go back to the bar to see if her friends are still there and have them come get her? Do I let her sleep it off? Do I . . . *fuck.*

Something that was supposed to be uncomplicated has now turned more than.

With a quick walk back to the bathroom, I roll the unused condom off my now limp cock and throw it in the trash. Next, I find my pants, pull them on, before approaching the bed and removing Scarlett's heels one by one, then moving her into a more comfortable position on the bed. Then I cover her with the comforter and stand there trying to figure out what to do next.

Get some work done while she sleeps it off? Fall asleep on the couch and deal with her in the morning? Go in the bathroom and jerk off and pretend?

The couch it is.

I'm not only unsatisfied, but now I'm suddenly exhausted. A long flight interrupted by a delay. A plate that's more than full with an NFL quarterback who I'm trying to help get caught up to speed on his new team's plays. A hothead MLB pitcher who got himself in trouble when he threw a punch at his catcher and oops, it just so happened to be caught on camera. Sure, it's my everyday wrangling of personalities, but currently, the load is heavier than normal.

Add to that list coming to Vegas where I do *not* want to be right now. *And Carson Vega is the last person I want to meet tomorrow.*

But I'm a man of my word.

Especially when my mentor and the man who got me started in this competitive, ruthless, all-encompassing business of sports management is calling to cash in a long overdue IOU. An IOU that I really don't have the time or desire to fulfill, but he is the one person who helped me gain my footing so I could be sitting where I am today.

Then again, that's not saying much considering my current circumstances—sitting here with a woman in my bed instead of being on top of her.

And yet, I still owe him. More than I could ever repay, really.

The question is, is corralling his current client a fair trade for my debts?

I've seen the online posts, and frankly I don't have time to deal with a prima donna, wild child. And that's exactly what Stevie Lancaster appears to be by all accounts on social media as of late. She may be the best female tennis player in the past five years, but I don't have time for her shit nor her drama.

But I'll humor Carson. I'll listen to his spiel, then tell him I don't have the space on my client roster nor the time and patience to motivate Stevie to behave and get back on track.

Scarlett laughs. She's still asleep and it's a sleep-drugged slur, but she laughs in a way that has me regretting how this night ended.

With a sigh, I grab one of the extra pillows off the bed and am just about ready to make myself comfortable on the couch when something from our conversation earlier ghosts through my mind. *This isn't a game and I'm not a con artist.*

"Shit," I mutter as I push back up and look at my wallet on the desk beside my laptop and tablet. What if she is one and this is all a game? It was convenient timing for her to pass out. For all I know, her friends are sitting down the hallway waiting for me to fall asleep to come in and rob me blind. After all, what else makes men go blind to what's going on around them than the idea of sex?

Paranoia getting the best of me, I grab everything I have of value in my room—including my key card—and place it in the hotel-provided safe in the closet.

And then of course, I feel like an idiot. But if Karma is a real thing, I best err on the side of caution.

I glance one last time at the woman sleeping in my bed before sinking onto the couch and falling asleep with my cell phone tucked into the waistband of my pants.

Chapter SEVEN

Finn

12 years ago

"Can you blame him for benching your ass?"

I don't lift my head from where it hangs, staring at the helmet in my hands between my knees. "Not now, Dad."

"Not now?" he snorts. "If not now, then when exactly? After Coach has kicked you off the team for your piss-poor effort on the field? After you've lost your scholarship and you have to pay for your own damn education? You're not exactly the most dependable son, so the last thing you need is to have your future depend on your own friggin' shoulders."

Shame washes over me in a way I've grown accustomed to when it comes to him and his outbursts. It doesn't matter how many times I've asked him not to come to the games, he still shows up. Still makes his way onto the field somehow after the game to broadcast his in-depth thoughts of how shitty I played.

"This is the ticket to your future, Finn. The NFL. A guaranteed paycheck to cash in for life."

I take a deep breath and consider my reality. My knees ache constantly, and the rotator cuff surgery I need has already decided my NFL future. *There won't be one.* But that's all I've ever been pushed to be. All I've ever been allowed to be.

"You know who that man is over there talking to Mason?" My father drones on despite the fact that I haven't spoken a word in response to him yet. "That's Carson Vega. One of the best sports agents in the business." He steps closer and leans down to whisper in my ear and it takes everything I have not to push him away. "He was here watching your team play today and now he's talking to your backup, Mason, instead of talking to you. You want to know why, son? Because you couldn't throw for shit today, so Coach pulled you. He benched you when what could be the most important man in your life was standing there taking notes on the game."

"Not now, Dad."

"Sports is the only thing you've ever loved. Now you've just thrown your career down the fucking drain by not performing at your peak when the best in the business has his eyes on you. Step up to the fucking plate, Finn."

I glance up for the first time since my dad walked over, to focus on someone other than him, and startle when I realize Carson Vega himself is only feet from us—within hearing distance. And of course, I want to crawl in a hole and die from embarrassment when his eyes meet mine. He offers a polite smile and nod before glancing to my side where my father remains bent over like a parent scolding a small child.

"I've got to get in the locker room. Coach's talk and all that," I mutter and rise from the bench without looking at my dad when I damn well know Coach is across the field still chatting with the media.

But it's a good excuse to get away from him.

A good out.

Anything to buy me time so that I can drown myself in alcohol later with the guys and forget today ever happened.

The shower is hot, the guys are rowdy over the win we secured once I left the game, and I drag my feet leaving the locker room. The last thing I want to do is go to dinner with my dad and listen to him break down every play, highlight every error, and tell me what I should have done.

Pushing the door to the locker room open, I keep my head down and don't care that my mood is shitty.

"Sanderson."

I startle at my name and then stop walking when I see Carson Vega five feet from me. He's leaning casually against a short concrete wall, arms crossed over his chest, one ankle crossed over the other. His dress shirt is crisp even after being in the hot sun during the game, his sleeves are rolled up at the cuff, and from what I gather, a very expensive watch is on his wrist. His dark hair is styled but not stiff, and as he's taken his sunglasses off, they're hooked in the top of his shirt.

"Sir?" I say, my heart pounding. I'm stuck in that moment between excitement over him actually talking to me and mortification over whether or not he heard what my dad said to me earlier.

"Carson Vega," he says in a smooth voice framed by a genuine smile as he reaches out to shake my hand.

"Finn. Uh, Finn Sanderson."

"I know who you are," he says and that has my heart lurching into my throat. "You've had a tough go of it lately. Your shoulder's damaged but you're waiting for the off-season to have surgery so no one knows how bad it is. Am I right?"

How did he know when I've told no one? Not even my dad. *Especially not my dad.*

My expression must have given my thoughts away because compassion fills his eyes. "You hitch your arm slightly before you go to throw," he says by way of explanation. "You're trying to hide it so you don't upset Coach, and your doctor has said you won't cause any more damage by playing so you're doing just that."

"How—"

"It's my job to watch and observe and know. And I've seen it more times than I care to count." He shrugs and glances down the corridor where someone yells something before looking back at me. "You'll get the surgery, you'll rehab, and you may or may not be back. Sometimes it works and you come back better than new, other times it's a shitshow and you realize your dream is gone. Not being harsh, but that's just how it goes."

I swallow over the lump of emotion that for some reason is lodged in my throat. Maybe it's relief that someone other than me knows about what I've been trying to hide. Maybe it's feeling like I'm not so fucking alone with this secret anymore. *Or maybe it's because he's not ripping into me, telling me what a fuck-up I am.*

"I've been asking around about you while you were in there." He lifts his chin to the locker room doors I just came out of. "You've got decent grades, have a strong work ethic or so Coach Tejada says, and more than anything, you've made yourself the go-between for your teammates with the coaching staff. I like that." He chuckles. "I like that a lot."

"Thank you," I say awkwardly, uncertain what one has to do with the other or where this conversation is going.

"Anyway, the reason I waited for you is I wanted to tell you this: your old man is wrong." My heart sinks at his words because, of course, I was hoping he was waiting to tell me he was interested in me. For the future. In representing me for the NFL. "I couldn't help but overhear what he said, and I don't know your dynamic, don't care to really, but in all honesty, what he said was bullshit. Just because you might not continue your career into the NFL doesn't mean your life in sports is over."

I open my mouth to make an excuse for my father but for what feels like the first time in my life, the words don't come out. Carson's words resonate that deeply with me. Instead, I shut my mouth and simply nod at this hulking presence in front of me.

Carson fishes in his shirt pocket and holds out what appears to be a business card. I take it without looking at it.

"You graduate with your degree, and if you're still interested in that career in sports, you come see me. I always need a good intern. Besides," he says, pushing himself off the wall and smiling, "you never know where that might lead."

And without another word, he begins to walk down the corridor.

"Mr. Vega," I call after him. He stops and turns to look at me as I hold the business card up. "Thank you."

He nods and then heads the other way. I watch him until he turns past the next building as I flip the card over and over in my hand.

Carson Vega just offered me an internship.

A lifeline.

A way to be a part of sports when I graduate.

Holy shit.

Maybe my life won't be as fucked up as I thought—or rather as my dad thought—after all.

Chapter
EIGHT

Finn

MY NECK IS KILLING ME.

That's my first and only thought when I slowly begin to wake up.

That and then the sudden jolt as something starts vibrating against my cock.

Phone.

It's my phone.

Why is my phone in my pants?

And before the thought even finishes in my mind, my brain fires, and last night comes back to me. *Scarlett.* Almost sex. Her passing out. Con woman.

Jumping off the couch, I cringe at the bright light streaming in the room from the curtains I didn't close. I hiss out a curse when my shin connects with the coffee table but the pain is quickly forgotten when I see my empty bed in front of me. The bathroom door is open, and the inside is empty. No Scarlett. She must have woken up and left.

That's when I see the four one-hundred-dollar bills fanned across the nightstand. I do a double take as I walk toward it as if I don't really believe what I see.

She left me cash? As if I were an escort who she was paying for his services?

I'm not sure if I should be offended or flattered.

Or even how I should feel about it.

And that same thought rings through my mind three hours later as I walk down the long hallway on the top floor toward the penthouse suite that Carson has directed me to. It's been almost a year since I've seen him so my eagerness to catch up is a double-edged sword against what I already assume he's going to ask me.

What I'm going to politely decline.

At least I'll be able to do this all without Stevie knowing since a quick look at her website says she's slated to appear in an exhibition match tomorrow in Florida.

The door has the lock latch folded so that it's ajar and can be pushed open. I knock anyway, and when it's pulled open, I'm met with the prodigious Carson Vega. Just like that first time I met him, I'm taken with his presence.

Except now, his once dark hair is snow white, and a pair of trendy frames sit atop his nose. His midsection has definitely gotten a little rounder since the last time I saw him, but I know from experience that he'll tell me it's been earned from a life well lived.

"Finn fucking Sanderson. Aren't you a sight for these sore eyes of mine." The man who became more like a father to me than my own during my tenure with him—before he pushed me to go out on my own—pulls me in for a quick man-pat hug, before motioning for me to enter the room. "Son of a bitch, you look good. But then again, you always look good."

"Says the man whose tan looks like he's been sitting on a beach in paradise instead of working."

"Perhaps." He gives a coy shrug and runs his hand over his belly. "This has grown too, but can't complain, son. Our hard work isn't all for naught unless you stop and enjoy it every now and again. So tell me, have you been enjoying it?"

I walk over to the panoramic window and take in the strip. What seems to be so glamorous at night looks anything but in the daytime. The blinking lights fall flat, and the hotels are one concrete wall after another no matter how much you dress them up.

I turn to face Carson and his expectant eyes. "I will at some point. When I reach your level of success." I shrug, knowing I have but will always place him on a pedestal regardless. "Until then, I work."

His sigh is expected as we've had this conversation more than once. "What you need is someone to experience things with. Someone to twist your arm every once in a while, and get you out from behind your phone and laptop."

I nod out of respect and then smile. "Is this a matchmaking ad? Since when did you go to work for them?"

"Matchmaking is the last thing I'll ever do." He sighs. "This is more like life advice from someone who learned the hard way."

"Noted."

"So you say time and again and yet you never seem to actually do it." His sigh fills the space. "Look, I know you think relationships are bull-shit and yada yada, but when you find someone who understands you, it makes a world of difference."

"Dually noted," I mutter.

"You're not getting any younger."

"And now I definitely know you've hung up your agent shoes and now work in matchmaking." I shake my head, wondering when early thirties became old to him. "So is that why I'm here? To pick up all your clients that you're leaving behind as you head into this new career?"

"See? Case in point. I haven't seen you for a year and you want to jump right into business instead of catching up."

"You're deferring, Carson."

"Damn right, I am," he says and crosses his arms over his chest before smiling. "Wasn't your motto always business first, pleasure later?"

His laugh is deep and rich. "I taught you well, Finn. I taught you well."

"So? Let's do business first and then we'll catch up after if you're free." And maybe I'll be able to smooth over any hurt feelings when I tell him I can't babysit Stevie Lancaster.

"That we can do." But his pause after he speaks has me narrowing my eyes as he takes a few steps over to where he perches himself on the arm of the sofa and stares at me. "I don't know how else to say it other than *I need your help*."

Shit. That pause should have warned me he was going to come out swinging.

And he just did. When Carson Vega speaks, he means what he says, so his unabashed honesty and the serious look in his eyes, already have guilt swimming through me.

My chuckle isn't exactly full of humor. "Help with Stevie Lancaster, I presume?"

He nods, a sudden somberness to his expression now. "You ever met her?"

"Not that I recall, but you know how our life is." Lots of handshakes, lots of faces before you for only seconds at a time before you move on. "But no, I don't think I have."

"You'd know if you had," he says with a shake of his head. "The woman is a tornado, an earthquake, and a hurricane all mixed into one. And that was my description before her dad passed away. Now? Jesus. She—"

"Her dad?" I ask. The whole sports world knows her father passed away, but I'm looking for more information than I can get from the canned stories I'd see on SportsCenter before a tournament final.

"Liam Lancaster. Great guy. Single dad. Her mom left when she was young and so he basically devoted his life to his little girl," he says while I partition off the part of me who understands being abandoned all too well. I don't want to sympathize with a woman I don't have time to deal with. "He was a tennis instructor at some country club and one thing led to another and he turned his talents into molding her into one of the best there's ever been."

"Okay . . ." *So what does that have to do with me?*

"He was her coach, her agent, her keeper in all aspects. He didn't trust anyone with the most important thing in his life except himself."

"That kind of devotion can be a dangerous thing."

Carson nods. "Exactly. He contacted me years ago. We'd met by happenstance a few times over the years, but this particular time he asked for an official meeting with me. I wasn't sure what to expect really but then I was flabbergasted by his request. He asked if I would agree to watch out, manage, whatever you want to call it, Stevie if something were to ever happen to him." He looks down at his hands and shakes his head ever so subtly. "It was before she was of age, but the documents he had drawn up and that I signed, communicated that I would be her agent and representation if something were to happen to him or he became incapacitated."

"But she's of age now. She's more than able and capable to fire and hire who she wants as a manager or as representation."

He holds his finger up for me to be patient. "The next time I heard from him was earlier this year. He called me to let me know he was dying from pancreatic cancer. I was shocked and saddened because he was so young, but he made me promise that I wouldn't say a word of it to anyone—especially Stevie. He thought it was best she didn't know. That she loved him as he was instead of looking at him as sick and with a finite amount of time. I told him it was the wrong decision, but he was steadfast in it. Fast forward to his earlier-than-expected passing and not only was Stevie blindsided but she's livid with me because I knew her father was dying and didn't tell her."

"Christ." I sigh the word out, feeling for Stevie on a human level but more than confused as to why Carson is giving me this long buildup before he gets to the point. He's not a long-winded man unless the last year has changed something. "I feel for her, Car, for the situation, but you know as well as I do that our responsibility as an agent is to suggest and guide and negotiate. If she's that pissed off at you that she's acting out, then let her go as a client and be done with her."

"She's not acting out because of me, son. She's acting out because even though Liam Lancaster was a demanding, unforgiving coach and manager, he was also her father and she doesn't know how to process his death."

"You're not a psychologist. You can't fix someone who doesn't want to be fixed. So I'll say it again, why not fire her as a client and be done with her?"

"I promised her dad I'd take care of her just like I once did the same *for you.*"

And there it is: the guilt trip, the unspoken IOU. The man who mentored me in my career—in my life—is asking for a favor.

But when he meets my eyes, all thoughts have stopped dead in their tracks. I've known Carson for a decade and have seen that look on his face only a handful of times. Most memorable was when he was looking at me the first time we met.

A look that says for some reason the person has touched him and this salty, old bastard will move heaven and hell to help them.

And I know before this conversation carries on any further that I'm going to say yes. Damn it to hell.

But where would I be without that look? Who the hell knows, but it definitely wouldn't be here—one of the top sports management agents in the game.

I force a swallow over the fact I haven't accepted yet and nod in a silent acknowledgment of all he's done for me.

"You say she's livid with you, Carson, then why hasn't she fired you?"

"Because she's never really had to make those kinds of decisions for herself. Her job was to play and his job was everything else. I'm here because, thank God, she trusts her dad's judgment even now that he's gone."

I rise from the seat and shove my hands in my pockets as I take in the strip again. People mill about here and there while the pool on the rooftop of one of the hotels within eyesight is teeming with bikini-clad women.

I wonder if Scarlett is down there, coming onto the next man she sets her sights on. It's easier to think about her and the what-could-have-beens than to admit to myself I'm being roped into this.

Shaking the thought from my head, I turn back to Carson. Better to just get it all out on the table. "What are your main concerns?"

"She's one of the most gifted tennis players I've ever seen, Finn, but she's drowning."

"Drowning?" I ask even though I've seen the pictures. The drinking. The acting out. The sudden about-face. "Or sowing her wild oats because she's been restricted for so long?"

"Perhaps a bit of both. What's important is that while she's refusing to accept her father's death, she's also taking wide liberties with her 'grieving' to the point that she's possibly ruining her career."

"But why *you?* Why do you care so much what happens to her when you pass taking in new clients daily?" I ask but then cringe the moment the words are out. I already know why, and I'm so preoccupied with Scarlett and feeling like my arm is being twisted that I didn't stop to think before I spoke.

His wince shows me I'm right.

"Because something about her reminds me of my Sadie." His voice is soft, his eyes solemn, as he recalls his daughter who passed away in her teenage years. "And as a father, I understand Liam Lancaster and his reasoning behind all he did."

I nod and ask again. "Carson, why am I here?"

"Because you're good at controlling the out-of-control," Carson states. "And Stevie is out of control."

"So, *what?* You're going to hand her over to me for representation? Sure, I can ink some new endorsement deals for her when and if she decides to chill out." And earn a pretty penny in commission off the out-of-control princess while I'm at it. "Not a problem."

"I need a little more than that."

"A little more than *that?* What exactly does *that* mean?"

"Stevie's burned some bridges in the past few months. She's skipped appearances, ditched some charity tournaments, even no-showed filming a Nike commercial. *Twice.*"

"And?" I cross my arms over my chest.

"She's pissed off a lot of people. People she shouldn't have pissed off, including the head of the US Tennis Association."

"Go on," I say.

"After her exhibition on Friday, I've set up a few goodwill events to attend over the coming weeks. In the old days we'd call it a bus tour, but you kids these days all take those private jets so . . ." He waves a hand away as if it's something he doesn't quite understand. "She comes from a generation I don't understand."

"I don't think your version of self-absorbed is different to hers, Car."

Carson's laugh says he pretty much agrees but is too much of a gentleman to put it into words. Instead, he acts like I never said the words at all. "I'm not sure what exactly to call it other than a goodwill tour."

He's playing down her antics. Fucking great.

"So her PR person will escort her to each event, make sure she shows up to do the song and dance, and all will be good," I say trying to negate whatever he's going to throw at me next.

"Except she'll walk all over a PR person. She'll charm them. Manipulate them. Give them the slip, and while the PR rep is busy lying that Stevie had to cancel last minute because she isn't feeling well, pictures will pop up all over social media showing otherwise. It's happened. She's done it. I need someone I can depend on. Someone who I trust implicitly to hold her hand until she comes to her senses and decides her career isn't worth ruining."

"I'm not a babysitter, Carson. I'm an agent with a full client list and—"

"And a reputation for handling difficult ones at that."

"Handling, yes. Handholding, no."

"I've told Carson I don't need a babysitter, a handholder, someone to keep me in check, or someone to tuck me into bed at night. In fact, I don't need anyone," a feminine, annoyed voice says as she stalks into the suite. By the time I turn to see who it is, her back is to me, and she's already heading toward the refrigerator and grabbing a water. A mane of blond hair hangs down her back and sways in tempo with her hips. "So don't waste your time, boys."

There is a small *crack* as she breaks the seal on the water before she turns around to face us, a smirk on her lips.

"Either of you boys want a drink?" She looks from me to Carson and then back to me. "No? Didn't think so."

The same smirk I saw last night.

The same lips I saw last night.

Motherfucker.

Chapter NINE

Finn

I KNEW SHE REMINDED ME OF SOMEONE WHEN WE MET IN THE BAR, but I couldn't place her, couldn't figure out who it was.

The brown wig she obviously wore didn't help matters either.

But there she is in full living color—Stevie fucking Lancaster. The same woman who lay in my bed last night with nothing but silk and lace and a soft snore.

And today? Today her cheeks are still flushed, but this time it looks like it's from the sun. She has a white, flowy cover-up over her bathing suit that's tied around her neck. It's obvious she's already been for a swim because it's wet where her tits rub against the thin fabric.

Sure, she's covered in all the right places, but the sight of those wet spots only serves to stir my imagination—or rather the exact knowledge of the smell of her skin and the feel of those lace-clad nipples against my tongue.

Then there are those lips of hers. The ones that are shocked into the shape of an O as she stares at me with eyes wide in surprise. She glances over to Carson like a kid caught in a candy store before she looks at me again.

But for me, the shock has faded to a confused anger. She left money— *paid me*—as if I was her whore. Fucking hell, and now Carson thinks it's best if I'm the one who holds her hand?

"Sounds to me like you leave a lot of things unfinished and just maybe you do need the handholding," I say with a quirk of my eyebrow, the innuendo not subtle in the least.

"I finish things just fine if they're worth my while. Maybe you should worry yourself with your own clients instead of butting your nose into my business." She doesn't break from my stare, the challenge a gleam in her eye.

Carson clears his throat. "Seems to me you two are off to a fabulous start. Finn Sanderson, this is Stevie Lancaster. Stevie, this is Finn."

"Finn, *huh?*" she says as she looks me up and down as if she's never seen me naked before. "He's who you brought in here to handcuff me?"

Images ghost through my mind of her and handcuffs, which don't really belong in the moment.

"I brought Finn on board because he's well versed in getting athletes back on track after they take a break for one reason or other," Carson says in a tone I've never heard from him. It's not annoyed but rather . . . more exhausted than anything.

And maybe it's me being the selfish prick I normally am but how did I not notice how tired Carson looks? How was I so wrapped up in anger at being summoned here that I didn't look close enough to see the bags under his eyes and the fatigue etched in the lines of his face?

"Back on track?" She snorts.

"Yes," Carson continues. "We were just sorting through the specifics, but he's going to be your right-hand man over the coming weeks. I've set up a series of events leading up to the US Open that you'll attend in addition to training."

"Jesus, Carson," she groans and all but stomps her foot like a petulant child. "I'm going to be training for the Open. The last thing I need is to be traipsing around shaking hands and kissing babies."

"Please. Continue," I speak for the first time. "Because you sound so very grateful for the opportunities you've been afforded. The ones you seem to be intentionally throwing away as of late."

"You don't know shit about me or my opportunities," she spits out as she turns all her fire and brimstone on me. "And I've worked my ass off to have them so, take your judgment and shove it up your ass, *kindly.*" Her smile drips with the same sarcasm her words do.

"No judgment here. But your father hired Carson because he clearly trusted him to do what was best for you. He's doing just that setting up this goodwill tour. So you'll go to every event. You'll train every day and get ready for the Open. And you'll do it all with me by your side every step of the way."

I want to choke over the words, but at the same time, I find a small pleasure in the disdain registering in her expression. She was clearly listening outside the door before she entered the room and expected me to balk at Carson's request.

I was too.

But now? Now I might have just taken an ounce of pleasure in watching her stiffen at my words. That's not saying I have a clue how I'll manage my current workload and babysitting her . . . but I'll deal with it somehow if the reward is putting her in her place somewhat.

We all jump when the ringer in Carson's phone breaks the silence-filled tension in the room. "Carry on. I have to take this," he murmurs as he holds his finger up and moves to the other side of the room.

Stevie huffs. "As I've said over and over and over again, I don't need a babysitter. I'm a grown woman who is just blowing off some steam as us grown-ups are allowed to do."

I pick up my phone and enter #StevieLancaster in the search bar on Instagram. My screen fills with picture after picture of her antics and debauchery over the past few weeks. Drunken selfies. Her trying out a stripper pole somewhere. Middle fingers held up to the photographer. Dancing in a nightclub clearly enjoying herself with the men on either side of her. "Clearly you do," I murmur as I hold up my phone to show her the endless supply of evidence. "Because *this*? This doesn't look like you're playing tennis to me."

"Like you follow tennis."

My chuckle is low and unflinching. "I don't have to follow tennis to know you look like a Kardashian mixed with Lindsay Lohan at her lowest in these pictures."

Her eyes narrow as she glares at me. "I spent time with the

Kardashians last month. For the record, we had a blast." Condescension drips from her words.

"Seems like a good enough reason to miss the opening of the Indio Springs tournament."

"I had a pulled groin muscle."

I flick through more pictures and find one dated before the Indio Springs tournament. Stevie is on a dance floor somewhere with drinks in both hands and her head thrown back. "Clearly your pulled groin was from twerking too hard."

"You're an asshole."

"No one disputes that, but then again, an asshole might have treated the nearly naked woman who passed out in his bed last night entirely different, *Scarlett*."

"I have no idea what you're talking about." Her smile is smug.

"Are you in the habit of leaving cash for the men you sleep with? Because if that's the case, we have a lot more shit to deal with than just your partying." I challenge, eyes locked on hers without a flicker of emotion on my face.

I don't know why I get a rise out of pushing her buttons but I do. She paid me like I was her whore and now in an unexpected twist of fate, I'll be the one getting paid to hold her feet to the fire.

And it'll be a lot more than four hundred dollars, I can assure you.

She glances over her shoulder to where Carson is still on his phone before staring at me, teeth gritted and anger firing in those green eyes of hers. "No, but perhaps I was paying for the hotel room I ended up occupying since its owner didn't exactly get to sleep in the bed himself."

Her words surprise me when I don't want them to. A sliver of decency in the overbearing wild-child façade.

Chapter
TEN

Stevie

SURPRISE FLICKERS ON HIS FACE AND I TAKE THE MOMENT TO WALK toward the window and look down at the pool party I'm missing. Carson's still talking on the phone, and I'm even more desperate to get out of this hotel room.

And then there's Finn. The prospect of Finn being my keeper does make things more than interesting, but the last thing I need is the man I was going to have sex with last night as my babysitter.

I mean, it's one thing to know you're walking into a meeting where you're most likely going to be corralled and caged back into your disciplined life. It's a whole other thing to find out the man who's been chosen to be your keeper is the same man who elicited from you the strongest orgasm of your life.

Shock. Anger. Confusion. Denial.

All four of them jolted through me as I all but choked on that first drink of water when I realized Rhett was who Carson had brought in. When I understood that Cards O' Fun just backfired in a major way with me being the butt of the joke.

A joke I'm going to try to find my way out of right now.

Talk about complicating things.

And making it more than awkward.

When I turn back around, his attention is focused on me. I study him. This time it's without the haze of alcohol or the thrill of a contest humming through my veins. It's sober and without a dare hanging over my head.

And damn, he's just as handsome as he was in the bar last night. Even more so.

"This is how you want to spend your time?" I ask him with one eyebrow raised. "I wouldn't want to take you away from your busy schedule and important client list. I'd think this babysitting job would have you losing money and we can't have that now, can we?"

He folds his arms over his chest and studies me in a way that is completely innocent but that heats my blood. "It's impolite to talk about money, Stevie. You should know that by now. Besides, how do you know I have a busy schedule or a long list of clients?"

"Because Carson is very thorough—painstakingly so—and he wouldn't have you here unless you had both."

He nods. "Very true."

"I'm just trying to figure out how exactly you plan to reprimand me if I step out of line." I take a step toward him and lower my voice much like he did because hell, two can play this game and I'm about to play winner takes all. "I'd think it's pretty hard to reprimand someone once you've had your fingers in them."

I have to give it to Finn. The shocked expression I was hoping for doesn't appear. He doesn't flinch but rather coughs out a laugh and gives a shake of his head as he takes a step toward me.

"I know your type," he murmurs just loud enough so I can hear it. "The good girl begging to be bad but not quite sure how to do that. The revered athlete who is itching to live a little when all she's had is one practice after another, with structure and schedules her entire life. The grieving daughter who's pissed at her dad for dying and is lashing out at the world to show them she's nothing like they thought she was to get back at him in some sick, satisfying way. Yeah, I know you, Stevie Lancaster. You're all about shock value. Anything to push away the people who are trying to help you the most." He glances over to Carson and then back to me with a smug smile on his lips, while I try to process him and everything he's saying that's too close to the truth and way more than I want to admit to. "Newsflash, Lancaster. You think that subtle reminder from last night will stop me from doing my job, and yet it just makes me want to do it more, even if it's just so I can piss you off."

"So you'd take this job just to piss me off?" I narrow my brow and put my hands on my hips, needing something—*anything*—to say while I hear and reject everything he's just said.

What kind of jerk knows someone less than twenty-four hours and thinks he has them pegged?

He doesn't know me.

No one does.

One man did, but now he's gone, and I will keep doing anything I can to avoid that pain. That loss. *That loneliness.*

"Big, bad sports agent thinks he can swoop in and save the day. I bet you're agreeing to this simply to boost your ginormous ego after it was bruised so badly last night. I mean it says a lot about a man when the woman he's with would rather fall asleep than have sex with him."

His grimace is barely noticeable but it's there. "Funny how you insult to redirect away from you. Classic avoidance. You might need to work on that because I wasn't born yesterday and can see right through your shtick." He chuckles. "You passed out because you were so busy trying to be something, *someone*, you're not. You better thank God it was my room you passed out in because another man might have taken what you offered even when you weren't coherent. Especially after you came all over his fingers."

There's a bite to his tone, a warning that I've overstepped, and there's something about his words that sends a chill down my spine. A chill that says I know he's right, that so much worse could have happened, but I refuse to let him know that.

"The god complex. Yes. I was waiting for that to make its appearance. Good to know you're like every other guy I've ever met before." Done with him and this conversation, I pull my phone out of my pocket and start skimming my social media. When he snatches my phone from my hand, I say, "*Hey!*"

"Better get used to it since it seems we're going to be attached at the hip over the upcoming weeks."

"Screw you."

And now my words are out there, hanging between us. The literal ones I tried to act on hours ago.

His smirk says he's on the same train of thought. "We could always try that again but I don't exactly think that's what Carson had in mind when he asked me to get you back on track."

Smug bastard.

But his eyes are still hungry when they look at me, and I may take small satisfaction in that.

"Then tell Carson you won't do it. Tell him you're busy. Tell him anything and save us both from having to deal with each other." I punctuate my words with a sweet smile.

"I can't." He glances over to Carson again.

"Yes, you can. You're a grown man. What could he possibly have to hold over your head to make you say yes?"

"I was once a defiant brat like you and Carson saw something worthy in me to help. Much like he does you for some unknown reason. That's why I'm staying. Not because I think you deserve it or even want to, but because I'm repaying a long overdue debt. Got that?"

Fury consumes me. Agents all over the world *want* to work with me, would give their eye teeth to work with me, and this asshole calls me a *brat*?

"Just for the record, *Rhett*," I spit the name at him. "You were right. Last night *was* a game, nothing more than a dare of sorts, and lucky me pulled the one-night-stand card."

"Card?" He lifts a lone eyebrow.

"You just happened to be in the right place at the right time. I never would have looked twice otherwise. I'm just super competitive and refuse to lose."

"So that's what you call it when you strip for a virtual stranger after exchanging no more than a quick conversation? Being competitive?"

I stare at him with my mouth open and then close it. I guess he's not afraid to play either. "You're—"

"So I see you two are getting along just fine," Carson says. We both startle and look his way, uncertain how long he's been standing there listening.

Finn chuckles softly and gives a shake of his head before his eyes leave mine and his attention turns to Carson. "I was just letting Stevie know how I operate."

"Jesus." Carson laughs. "Don't scare her away just yet."

"He doesn't have to scare me away, Car, because this isn't going to happen. Like I told you, I'm a grown woman who—"

"Who is acting like a petulant child," Finn finishes for me. "A teenager who is getting way too much press for her antics off the court rather than on it. A woman who seems determined to throw away some of the best talent I've seen in a long damn time. So you can stand there and pretend that's exactly what you want, or you can step up to the fault line and figure your shit out."

I start to cross my arms over my chest and then stop when I realize that only serves to reinforce the broad stroke he just painted me with.

"I've got shit to do," I mutter and start to stalk out the door.

"Like practicing with Kellen?" Carson asks. "The court is reserved and he's waiting."

I snort in response.

"I'll see you after practice," Finn says as I grab the handle. "In the meantime, Carson and I are going to lunch to discuss my level of involvement in your affairs and where we go after the exhibition match this week."

His words stop me.

"Excuse me?" I turn to face him and would love to knock that smug, cocky smirk off his lips.

"We start now, Stevie. No more dicking around."

"So just like that, you two men get to discuss me as if I were your property?"

"Someone has to since you haven't seemed capable of claiming it as of late," Finn says.

"Are you kidding me?"

"Not in the least," Finn murmurs while Carson's expression softens for the first time, almost as if he might suddenly feel sorry that he's sicced Finn on me. "But please, keep up the spoiled-brat routine because it makes my job that much more exciting. When you act like a grown-up, I'll start treating you like one."

I turn on my heel with an exaggerated huff and slam the door behind me.

Or at least I try to but that damn metal lock bar is still across the jam so there's no satisfying *slam* of the door, only a clang against metal.

I stalk down the hallway toward my room, my thoughts flying and my temper raging.

Finn Sanderson thinks he's better than me?

Maybe I'll show him he's not. Maybe I'll make his life so miserable that he wants nothing to do with me.

But then again . . . wouldn't Finn—good looking, great-kisser Finn—be a much better babysitter than Carson or whoever the fuck else he'd pick to handcuff me to?

This is a no-win situation.

Clearly.

And while I have no one to blame but myself, that doesn't mean I have to go down without a fight.

Chapter

ELEVEN

Finn

"What's she like?"

"Who?" I ask as I glance up at Greg, my fresh-faced intern, who's standing in my office doorway as I collect everything I think I'll need over the coming weeks.

"Stevie Lancaster."

I stop and stare at his expectant gaze. The kid has a crush on her. It's written all over his face. While my male clients definitely outweigh the number of female clients I have, few and far between look like Stevie.

"Currently she's a train wreck, which is why I'm being sent in to fix the situation."

"Why you?"

"Because of Benji Garrison and Hank Thompson and Jonny Barnes and—"

"So basically, because you deal with troubled clients and turn them around?" he asks, inferring from the list of players I offered. The players who had screwed up their careers majorly somehow, or were trying to, and how I came in and straightened them out.

"Apparently," I grumble, putting my hands on my hips as I survey my office. The last thing I expected Carson Vega to do during our lunch earlier today was play hardball. Not that I didn't know it was in him, but not with me, an agent trying to help him out.

I thought he'd say I was to meet Stevie at her next event. *Next week.* That I was to head back to New York and get my shit in order before heading out on the road with her over the coming weeks.

Little did I expect that her first public appearance was tomorrow afternoon and that he required me to be there guiding it.

I was given twenty-four hours. Twenty-four fucking hours to return home and then back to Vegas ready to play nanny.

I told Carson no. I told him it was impossible. I told him I had shit to take care of.

Then of course, he wrote a six-figure number on a napkin and slid it across the table that had me doing a double take before he said, "That's how much this kid means to me. Don't screw it up."

At least he's making it worth it. I guess the coffers run deep when it comes to her. The downside of the deal is that I have to spend the next six weeks holding her hand while doing my day-to-day work. The upside? She's definitely better looking than the rest of the clients I have to work with.

"So?" Greg asks.

"Go away, Greg."

"Ah, c'mon, man. She's on my island. The least you can do is let me know if she's as pretty in person as she is online. If she smells good. If she's nice. That kind of shit."

His words have thoughts and images flashing through my mind of Stevie against the wall and my mouth on hers. Her smell. Her taste. Her moans.

Forgetting about the night might be a tad harder than expected when I'll be faced with it on the daily. But I don't date female clients. I don't fuck female clients. I don't get overly friendly with any clients. That was the first lesson that Carson taught me during my tenure at Vega Management.

Distance is how you keep your nose clean and your reputation stellar.

So as tempting as it would be to finish what the two of us started, all bets were off when she walked in the room and was no longer

Scarlett from the bar but was Stevie Lancaster, the athlete Carson wanted me to manage.

"Your island?"

"Like if you were stranded on an island and could pick five women to have on it with you forever type of five. Stevie's one of my five."

"That's the stupidest thing I've ever heard. First off, why would you have only five? Why limit yourself?"

"That's the rules."

"Whose rules? Why not just break the rules, be smart, and don't get stranded? Seems pretty simple to me. Then you can have any woman you want. Life's too short to be strapped to any woman."

I look up from my desk at the utter confusion blanketing Greg's face. "Because that's not the rules," he repeats.

"Greg, here's the deal, sometimes you need to make your own rules. Sometimes you need to break a few now and again to change the situation you're in. It's the people breaking the rules who are the ones succeeding. So screw having just five. Don't get stranded at all and then you can have all the women you want."

"Yes, sir," he says and clears his throat, clearly uncomfortable with my commentary and advice.

"The whole theory implies that you could only get these women if you were stranded. Why not have the confidence that you could land them in everyday life?" I shove some papers in my briefcase and look back up at him. "Confidence is paramount in this career, Greg. Even if you don't think you can land someone, you have to pretend that you can. You have to fake it till you make it."

He stands there quiet for a beat as he shifts on his feet and frankly, I'm proud of myself for having this much patience. Normally I'd have run him off by now. But the poor kid is gangly and slightly clueless despite his more than impressive job performance since he's come on board.

"So you're telling me you think I'd have a shot at her?" he asks and it takes a second for it to register what he means and even longer for me to clear the shocked-as-shit look off my face.

Especially when his words feel like flint to my temper. It's a reaction I don't expect nor want. Stevie is nothing more to me than a client I don't want as a client.

"I'm telling you that she's a pain in my ass." *And no, you'll never have a shot with her.* "A royal one at that who I now have to babysit because she's determined to ruin herself or her career or perhaps both."

"I'd be glad to come and assist you."

"I'm sure you would." I chuckle. "I'm sure you would."

Chapter

TWELVE

Stevie

"Better but you're still off. You need to add more lift to the racket."

I think I'm going to die.

"You're not getting to the ball fast enough. Speed up your footwork."

Screw you, Kellen.

But aren't I the one who's screwed? Aren't I the one who was seeded in the top five in the world only to now feel out of shape and off my game?

There's no one else to blame but yourself.

I shove the thought away as I gulp in air. Isn't a girl allowed to grieve? Isn't she allowed to fail a little in the process?

At the same time though, the women I chased down on the court, beat, and then outranked are now breathing down my neck. Are now threatening to take that rank I worked for back.

"C'mon, Stevie. Get there," he shouts as he hits one to the corner of the court that is just beyond the reach of my racket. His hiss of disappointment is a loud echo in my head that piles on top of the dissatisfaction I feel everyone has with me these days. *Freaking par for the course.*

I hold up a middle finger to him as I gulp water, and his laugh reverberates around the empty court. The last thing I need is to be lectured right now. Dare I say I'm actually enjoying myself?

The squeak of my shoes on the court. The jolt to my forearms when I hit the ball in the sweet spot. The burn of my muscles as I repeat the same stroke over and over. The satisfaction of the ball landing perfectly just inside the line.

At least the indoor tennis courts provide us with air conditioning and cover from the sun or else I would be hurting on a much larger scale.

The problem is, even though I'm sucking major wind, there is peace in being here. A feeling of rightness. For the first time in weeks, I feel settled and maybe that's because I'm on the court. In the place I've always found comfort.

Where I feel closest to my dad.

It's also a double-edged sword because every time I look across that net, I expect to see my dad there. I expect to see his red hat and stern look that tells me I'm not working hard enough. I expect to hear "*Game on, Stevester*," in that gravelly voice of his that demanded more from me even when I didn't think I had more to give.

But somehow, I'd find it for him. Somehow, I'd dig deeper again and again until he'd give me that slight nod of his chin that told me he was satisfied. No words of praise, just that nod and—

"Again," Kellen says when I walk back to the fault line. Another ball comes at me to hit.

And then another.

I work tirelessly, ball after ball, shot after shot, backhand after backhand, with Kellen's name an endless curse on my lips and what I swear is alcohol sweating out of my pores.

It doesn't help that Vivi, Jordan, and I may have had a hotel room party where we drank a bit too much to celebrate the fact that Carson sent Finn back to wherever he's from for the night.

A small and unexpected reprieve that I took happily.

But now I'm paying for it. Big time.

Winded, nauseous, and clueless over how long we've been at it since there is no sun above to guestimate time, I lean over and brace my hands on my knees to catch my breath.

"Game on, Stevester. Let's go."

The words hit me like a ton of bricks.

Words that have been heard time and again on television during

Grand Slam finals. Ones spoken to me by my father, but *only* ever by my father.

Except for right now.

And hearing them stops me dead in my tracks.

I know it shouldn't bug me that Kellen is using them as a means to motivate, but . . . they were *his* words. *Only his.* Something no one possibly understands.

And hearing them right now only serves to shine a spotlight on the glaringly obvious hole that I now have to live with forever.

One I'm not even quite sure I've seen to the depths of yet.

The words cripple me when I don't want to be crippled.

"We're done," I pant out and walk over to the bench. I don't wait to see his reaction as I put my racket into its case and zip it up. I don't turn to face him as his footsteps come closer. All I can focus on is the anger vibrating through me and trying to contain it.

"You okay?" he asks, but I don't trust myself to speak so I just nod. "Your body is probably rebelling, correct? You haven't been treating it right so it's probably telling you to fuck off and die about now."

"Something like that," I murmur, suddenly needing to get out of this place and get some fresh air.

"You're looking decent, but we're going to have to catch up some. A month off is a long time to take off when—"

"It hasn't been a month," I snap at him. He's freaking crazy. There's no way—

"You're right. It's been five weeks," a voice says from the stands at my back. "Maybe even longer than that."

I turn to see Finn Sanderson standing there and immediately, my back stiffens in protest at his presence while other parts of me that I don't want to react, heat up.

He's the distraction I need and the perfect adversary to help take my mind off what Kellen just said and how I feel about it.

"And how would you know?" I place my hands on my hips and glare at him. "Keeping tabs on me before you knew me? Should I worry that you're secretly obsessed with me and that I need to fear for my safety?"

"No, you should worry about how your backhand is late and your serve isn't up to par, because you've been busy dicking around for the past five-plus weeks doing anything and everything to not prepare for the US Open."

"*Dicking around?* Interesting choice of words," I say and take a step closer to him, needing someone to feed off my need to forget.

His smirk is a flash, but it's there, and then gone just as quickly. "You'll learn I don't mince words."

"Good to know," I murmur, keenly aware that Kellen is still at my back, no doubt curious about this exchange. This is none of his business.

Then again, it seems my business is everyone's business these days.

And as if right on cue, Finn shifts his attention to Kellen. "How'd she do?"

"You could ask me directly," I interject.

"Now why would I do that when I can get an honest response from him instead of a bullshit one from you?"

I glance over to Kellen who is shifting his feet, trying to figure out this dynamic. "I look decent," I respond at the same time Kellen tries to speak. "I'm slow on my break and have a slight delay on my timing but it's all things that are fixable with repetition and training."

"And are you?" Finn asks as he pushes off the wall and takes a step toward me so that now he's in clear view, and I hate that for a brief second, I'm at a loss for words.

I've seen Finn in a tailored dress shirt the first night we met.

I've seen him in a polo shirt and jeans yesterday in Carson's suite.

Hell, I've even seen him butt-ass naked, but right now as he stands across the court from me in a perfectly tailored suit, there's something about him that has me reminding myself to breathe. He may be fully clothed but there's something about the way he wears his suit that has me recalling the feel of his naked chest beneath my palms. The feel of his hard length against my fingers. The taste of his kiss when I don't ever remember tastes of kisses nor do I want to.

Get a grip, Stevie. You don't like suits. You never have. You like men with tattoos and shaggy hair and a touch of the reckless thrown in. You like the rebel without a cause so that it and he doesn't interfere with your life.

You don't like *this*—styled, perfected, aloof. *Cold.* You're not attracted to *him*—driven, domineering, *demanding.*

Yet I'm staring at him stumbling over simple words and easy thoughts wondering, if I'm not attracted to men like him, then why did I pick him for my Cards O' Fun one-night stand then?

And more importantly, why are any of these thoughts in my head? That's probably the most important question.

"Stevie?" he asks. My name almost a taunt to tell him what I'm thinking so hard about.

"Yes? What?"

"I asked, *are you?*"

"Am I what?" I hate that I sound flustered, but I am.

"Are you going to put the work in?" He takes another step toward me, his question irritating because, what does he care?

"What's it to you besides a guaranteed paycheck?" I ask.

"I have plenty of guaranteed paychecks, so yours is just unexpected icing on the cake." His chuckle is low and discernable. "But after today, my name will be associated with yours so yes, it matters if you put the work in. I don't like to be made to look bad."

I snort. "Of course. Wouldn't want to make Finn Sanderson look shitty in the press's eyes even though I'm more than certain your halo is crooked most days."

"First, there is no halo. I never claimed to be a saint and I assure you I'm not. But I'm not the face-of-a-generation tennis player like you are. Second, you're goddamn right it's my reputation now attached to yours whether I want it to be or not. *Remember that.* Put the work in or else now you answer to me." Our glares hold for a stretch of time as the muscle in his jaw ticks. "Are we clear?"

I take back every single one of the thoughts I had seconds ago. He's not attractive. He's infuriating and frustrating and arrogant and Jesus Christ, how is this ever going to work with him being my shadow?

"Crystal," I grit out and grab my bag, hoisting it over my shoulder.

"Where do you think you're going?" he asks.

"Back to the hotel to meet up with my friends," I say, thinking of how I'm going to strangle Vivi and Jordan for Cards O' Fun and picking him for my dare. Without them, none of this would have misaligned the way it has. "I've put my time in here, have I not?" I glance over to Kellen but don't wait for his response. "And I will again tomorrow. For now, I'm off the clock."

"No, you're not."

"Excuse me?" I ask.

"I took the liberty to tell Jordan and Vivi that it would be best if they head back home. That—"

"You what?" I screech and stalk up to him, more than pissed. "Who the hell do you think—"

"You heard me." The lift of his eyebrows is a taunt all in and of itself. "I told them that you've all had your fun, and they could either be known in the media as the friends who helped destroy your career or the good friends who knew when to step away. They chose wisely."

"So you fucked them too?" I ask, my irrationality suddenly pulling the question out of the air without any basis other than pure, green jealousy. How did he know where to find them? How did he talk to them? How did—

"*Too?*" Finn steps in to me with temper flaring in his eyes. "That would imply I've fucked someone in the thirteen hours I've had to fly to New York, collect my shit, and get back here to babysit one pissy prima donna. I assure you, to my dismay, that I haven't. So watch what you say and who you say it to. Jealousy is a nasty bitch and it looks unbecoming on America's sweetheart." His eyes flicker over my shoulders where Kellen is slowly packing up our gear, definitely listening but pretending that he isn't.

"I assure you," I say using his words, "I'm nowhere near jealous."

He snorts in arrogant disbelief and leans in so that I steel myself for everything about him. His cologne. The warmth of his breath. The rumble of his voice. "For the record, Stevie, who I fuck is none of your business. Got that?"

I grit my teeth and stare at him with tears in my eyes, hating these weird feelings—confusion, jealousy, anguish—that are owning me right now. Feelings that don't make sense to me but that I feel nonetheless.

And I hate them.

I'm sick of feeling right now.

Sick of everything.

"Got it," I say smugly and start to walk past him, ready to be out of here and away from him.

He puts his hand on my arm and I yank it back. "Where are you going? We have plans," he says.

"I don't have any plans with you."

"That's where you're wrong." He lifts a hand to wave to Kellen. "Remember? I'm your babysitter. You go where I say you go. That's the perks of being in charge."

And when he takes my bag from my shoulder to carry it for me, he's lucky I don't take a swing at him with my other hand.

Chapter
THIRTEEN

Stevie

"What do you mean our hotel room?" I ask, looking dumbfounded as Finn makes himself comfortable on the couch in my hotel suite and props his feet up on the coffee table with a sigh.

"Today was a good start," he says completely ignoring my question. "You squeezed in a good practice, you had some great PR with the tennis academy, and then maybe made some reparations with Nike after that dinner we just had."

"Good. Great." I cross my arms over my chest and glare at him, knowing there is no way I just heard him correctly. "Now can you kindly explain what you meant when you said this was *our* hotel room?"

"As in ours. Yours and mine."

I shake my head as if to physically reject what he's saying. "What are you talking about? I know damn well you had a hotel room. I paid you money for it. Go sleep there."

He turns to me for the first time and that schmooze of charm he had all night with the Nike reps is now directed at me—albeit with condescension in it this time. "I can't sleep there because I checked out yesterday before I left. The money you so kindly left on my pillow to pay for my services was donated to the program for teens we went to today. And this suite has three rooms. One for you, one for me, and one for that giant, frustrating ego of yours so you can let it have a rest from how much overtime it's been working."

"No. The answer is no." I push his feet off my table and his chuckle in response only serves to anger me further.

"It's more efficient this way. It's only for a couple of days before your exhibition and then we move on to the next city, the next place, in our let's repair Stevie's image tour."

"I never agreed to that."

"You didn't have to. Carson had already set it up. You spent five weeks in the public eye undoing and distancing yourself from the person you were. Now we need to spend that same amount of time to get you back there."

But what if I don't want to go back there?

What if . . . what if I don't know what to want or how to feel or even where to look for that? I've spent my entire life under my dad's thumb—missing so much of normal life for this incredible life that I have—is it so wrong to want a little bit of both?

But I don't dare speak the words. I don't dare say what every single person would look at me like I'm crazy for.

"And let me guess, you're the one who is responsible to hold my hand during it all."

"I'm as thrilled about it as you are." He lowers his phone he was busy scrolling through and meets my eyes. "Are you always this irritable?"

"I've been called America's Tennis Sweetheart before. I don't exactly think that coincides with irritability."

"And yet that's all I've seen from you thus far."

"Apparently you bring this side out of me," I mutter.

"Good to know." He goes back to his phone and I go back to feeling completely dismissed. Antsy. Pissed that I didn't even get to say goodbye to Vivi and Jordan.

Angry at this man who sat beside me all afternoon while I made an appearance at a tennis program for underprivileged youth. To the one who often spoke for me during the dinner he'd scheduled with the marketing heads of Nike. To the man who is now occupying my hotel room.

I need some distance from him. A drink. Maybe even a bit of trouble to make me feel something.

"Oh my God. I forgot my purse." I don't intend to get in trouble when I utter the lie. It's more my need for space to think and process and be alone.

In a casino full of people.

Even I don't buy my own excuses and yet I still make them.

"I can go grab it," Finn says with a resigned sigh and begins to push himself off the couch.

"No. It's okay. I'll go." I take a step toward the door. "I don't feel good anyway and it's better if I walk it off."

"We can send one of your bodyguards to get it." He rises from his seat, pointing to the room next door where they are stationed.

"No. They don't know what it looks like." I grab a baseball hat I left sitting on the counter and pull it down over my forehead to help disguise myself. "I'll be right back."

I'm out the door of the suite before he can answer and all but jogging down the hall on my heels, the need to escape pressing on me with every step.

"Stevie!" Finn's voice calls to me down the hallway just as I step onto the elevator. "Your purse is right here."

Caught in my lie, I jab at the button to close the elevator door as his feet clod down the hallway.

"Goddammit," he groans when he tries to stick his hand in the just-closed door but it's too late. My squeal is loud and my laugh that follows makes me feel more alive than I've felt all night.

"Bye, Finn," I shout as the car starts to descend.

I get hung up on a few floors but my grin is wide the entire time as I picture Finn standing there in his shirt unbuttoned at the collar and my sparkly purse in his hand.

Might as well go have some fun before I head back and have to answer to him, because let's face it, I might have just screwed myself royally when it comes to Finn.

Sure, I'm on a slight high right now because, while I may have succeeded in getting out of the hotel room, now Finn will never trust me again.

I'll find a way to make him. To break him. To bend him to my will. Of that, I'm confident.

The elevator opens to the clink and clank and buzz of the casino. Stale smoke hangs in the air and the intermittent calls for "Cocktails" ring out around the floor. I take in the scene in front of me and decide to move toward the bar and indulge in one, solitary drink. Of course, I'll want more, but I'm going to be on my best behavior.

As it is, I'll have to go back and share the suite with Finn so it might be best to not be sloppy drunk when I face him. Besides, getting on the court today felt good. All except for the sucking wind part. I know the copious amounts of alcohol and bad food I've eaten over the past few weeks majorly contributed to that.

I wander through the casino, keeping my head low and my face in the shadows of the baseball hat. I'm sure people are wondering about my fashion statement—the fancy dress, the high heels, and the baseball hat—but it's Vegas after all. People are used to everything here.

I grab a drink. I play a few slot machines using the cash app on my phone to pay for it. The high of escaping Finn has waned and without Vivi or Jordan here, Vegas doesn't exactly feel like as much fun as it had.

"Hey. Sorry. I know it's late there," I say when Vivi answers the phone as I people watch from a darkened corner in the hotel bar.

"You know me. I'm always up." She pauses. "Everything okay?"

"I'm sorry about Finn. About him pushing you out. About not getting to say goodbye." I shrug even though she can't see it. "I feel bad."

"Don't. We had fun. Hell, we had the time of a lifetime . . . but now it's time for you to get back to what you do best. I just hope us being there helped some."

"It did. More than you'll ever know."

"Good. Now, I'd tell you to behave but a small part of me wants you to be a pain in the ass for Finn. *Just because.*"

"I may currently be doing just that." My smile is bittersweet. I'm already missing my friends, but I know she's right—that I need to get back to my everyday life.

"Good for you." Her laugh makes me smile.

"Love you."

"Love you too."

I stare at my cell for a few seconds before shaking my head and deciding to wander once again. I'm restless as I move through the casino, and I'm not sure if it's because I don't have Vivi and Jordan to keep my thoughts at bay or because I'm afraid to go back to the hotel room and face the consequences of my actions.

Both are equally crappy.

I yelp when I turn the corner and run smack dab into Finn. His eyes glint with a frustrated anger and his expression isn't much better as he grabs my bicep and holds me firmly in front of the casino's ticket booth for its big show.

"Christ, woman. You're infuriating," he grits out.

The sight of him knocks me from my funk and gives me exactly what I need—a sparring partner to take my frustration out on.

My smile is taunting, his words just what I want right now. "You like the challenge and you know it."

He snorts. "I like a lot of things, but chasing you through a hotel at this hour when my body is on East Coast time isn't one of them."

"Then what is it you do like, Finn?"

My words hang there as the doors open abruptly and people begin swarming out of the casino's theater. Finn and I are jostled to the side of the somewhat dim hallway so that we're all but pressed against the wall. His hand is still gripping my bicep, but it's his body now that is pressed against mine, bringing back thoughts and sensations from the other night.

Thoughts and sensations I can't ignore.

I don't know why I do it. Whether it's because I remember that I thought it would be fun to break him and have something to use against him or because I've thought about doing it way too much during the dinner tonight, but I rise on my tiptoes and lean in to press my lips to his.

But he holds me in place so that my lips are a whisper away from his. I can feel the warmth of his breath. Can feel the thunder of his pulse where he holds my arm. Can see the desire darkening in his eyes while we stare at each other in the suspended state of anticipation, as patrons bump against us as they pass by.

"Kiss me, Finn," I whisper just above the fray.

I know he hears me. It's in the quick intake of his breath and the reflexive squeeze on my arm as his eyes hold mine in a way that tells me he's contemplating doing just that.

"Finish what we started," I murmur, my lips just barely touching his with their movement.

I hold my breath, already tasting his kiss before it begins.

But it never happens.

His lips never meet mine and take what I thought we both wanted.

Instead, he releases my arm and steps back with a shake of his head. A shake that I can't seem to forget as I watch Finn Sanderson walk away and disappear into the casino crowd.

Chapter

FOURTEEN

Stevie

"Stevie, it's Ryan Churchill here. Hey, I hope you're doing well. I didn't realize you were shopping for an agent. Rumor is you're thinking of signing with Finn Sanderson. He's good for sure, but not someone I see you meshing well with. To be frank, he's not what you need at this point in your career and life. You need more guidance and less demand. Someone to help you through all of . . . what you have going on. I'd love to be the one to provide that for you. Maybe we can sit down and chat. I'd be happy to let you know how I operate."

I delete the voicemail as I walk into my suite and look at the four other numbers below it in my inbox, which no doubt sound much the same. I switch over to my texts and know just by the previews that the first six are more agents.

All of them are fishing to see if the rumor around town is true. I'm not even sure how it got out there but it's now being shared nonetheless.

I scan through the texts. Each one is an introduction. Each one is a reason I should look at them for representation. And the one other consistent inference in each and every one is that Finn is too harsh for me because apparently, I need coddling. *Coddling?*

Does everyone think I'm fragile and that I'm going to break?

Guess the word is out.

Stevie Lancaster has a new agent.

And apparently, she needs to be coddled and handled with kid gloves. *Or so they think.*

My dad was the one who always dealt with this side of the business. The day-to-day. The wheeling and dealing. Being my agent, my coach, my business manager, mentor all in one. All I had to do was get on the court and make whatever happened between the lines count.

Am I on the market? Do I want to be?

I glance over to where Finn sits at the desk in the suite. He's sitting with his back to me, typing away on his computer, his body framed by the darkening Las Vegas skyline. My dad picked Carson to take over for him in the agent department, so I have no reason not to trust his judgment since my father never steered me wrong before. And now Carson has picked Finn.

I'm still not sure how I feel about that—or rather, I know exactly how I feel about that—but I can't seem to separate his rejecting my request for him to kiss me two nights ago from whatever he seems so busy doing all the time as an agent.

Because let's face it, I've never been rejected by a guy before and it fucking sucks. The self-doubt that creeps in is worse than the rejection itself.

Am I not pretty enough? Sexy enough? *Anything* enough? Or does he simply see me as a child now?

"But please, keep up the spoiled-brat routine because it makes my job that much more exciting. When you act like a grown-up, I'll start treating you like one."

Why does his opinion matter?

Normally, you'd walk away from the person and never contact them again.

I can't.

In fact, I have to share a suite with the man who rejected me. I'm forced to look at his gorgeous face and be around him and his sex appeal when I don't want to. The deep rumble of his voice on the phone through the walls wakes me up as he talks to people on the East Coast. His fresh-from-the-shower scent trails him around the suite like a pheromone that dares me not to be affected. Everything about him reminds me of the taste of his kiss and the feel of his hands on my body.

But I don't like him. Not one bit.

Or at least I tell myself that.

It's just the challenge of him that makes me take note. Just the need to know why being with me the first night we met was acceptable but now a kiss isn't.

It's frustrating.

It's infuriating.

And to make matters worse or maybe better, depending on how you look at it, the man won't talk to me unless he has to.

Ever since I got lost in the moment and asked him to kiss me, he's been as aloof as aloof can be unless he's telling me what to do or answering a question from me clarifying what I need to do.

There hasn't been one mention of why he walked away. Nothing. Just a cold shoulder and complete disassociation.

The banter I rather enjoyed is gone.

The cut downs and comebacks nonexistent.

The innuendo that told me he still looked at me as a woman, forgotten.

I stare at Finn's broad shoulders and hear the clicking of his fingers over his keyboard and want to be noticed.

I drop my bag onto the floor with a thud.

He doesn't even stutter in his typing.

"Hey," I murmur.

He grunts in response, and I grit my teeth.

"How was your day?" I ask.

Nothing.

"I'm tired. That was a lot for one person to handle in a day," I try again.

"If you wanted to share the responsibility, then you either shouldn't have fucked off for the past month or chosen to play a team sport so you could blame others when you fail."

His words slap at me. "Wow. Okay. Let's try not to be a dick every waking moment of every day, shall we?"

"Noted." He glances over his shoulder at me and nods.

"What's your problem?" I ask, crossing the room and stepping in front of the desk so that he's forced to look at me.

"No problem at all. Why? Can I help you with something? Did you get yourself in trouble in the short jaunt from the training center to the hotel that I need to be aware of?" Everything about him—his posture, his expression, his tone—tells me he'd rather be anywhere else than here.

"I—no." I stand there until his fingers stop typing and he peers at me from over the lid of his laptop. "Why are you being this way?" I hate that my voice isn't stronger, that the tinge of hurt is woven through my tone, but it's out there and I can't take it back.

"Being what way?" he asks, completely tone deaf, when I know he sees my confusion.

"Nothing. Never mind," I say. "I'm going to take a shower."

I start to walk away when his voice at my back says, "I learned a long time ago not to get personal with clients."

My feet falter. *Honesty.* Finn's actually being honest. But that shouldn't make me . . . invisible. "Being decent and getting personal are two different things, Finn. I thought maybe we were starting to get along. That maybe we could make the best of this bad situation."

"And the other night in the casino was what?" he asks, voice still unemotional.

"You mean when you were willing to sleep with me or when you walked away from me? Because a few days doesn't change the situation all that much."

"If you don't like it, you can find another agent. I'm more than sure your phone is blowing up about it like mine is. I believe the clause in your contract with Carson is that you give him a written ninety-day notice. So even if you were wanting to change agents, you're still stuck with me for three months."

"Good to know you already looked at the clause on how to take the easy out." I swallow over the lump in my throat at what feels like more rejection.

"You're the one who seems unhappy." He shrugs as if I'm dismissed but his eyes hold mine, looking for what? *I don't know.*

"I'm not unhappy . . . I just . . . they all seem to think I need to be coddled."

"Do you?"

"Do I what?"

"Need to be coddled?" He lifts his brows and stares.

"No. Of course not."

He nods but his eyes tell me he doesn't believe a word I say. *Screw him.*

"Good. Welcome to the club, then." There's a self-deprecating chuckle that follows his words that I don't quite understand but when he turns his back to me this time, I know for a fact I'm dismissed.

FIFTEEN

Finn

"THIS IS STUPID."

A nod from Kellen that's neither in agreement nor disagreement but acknowledges that he hears her.

"I should have backed out."

The charity exhibition deemed Battle of the Sexes was supposed to be one for the ages. At the time it was booked, the game was pitting the number one men's seed, Ian Greshenko, against one of the top women's seed, one Stevie Lancaster. The goal was to raise money for Net Generation, a charity that promotes tennis in underprivileged neighborhoods, with the loser forfeiting their winnings to said charity.

Stevie's father thought not only would it be great publicity and raise money for Net Gen, but it might prove once and for all what he knew, that Stevie was better than the best man on the circuit.

But then Liam Lancaster died.

And she fell down whatever rabbit hole she fell into that I'm trying to help pull her out of.

On top of that, Greshenko is such a self-righteous prick who is known behind closed doors between us agents as someone we don't want to really deal with. Most men would see that Stevie is struggling in this exhibition that doesn't count for anything and would back off some.

But not Ian.

No, he's going in for the kill. He doesn't care that the crowd has paid top dollar for the seats and that maybe he should stretch the match out longer to let them get the most for their money. He only cares about himself and fueling his ego.

And it's not as if Stevie is playing horribly, not compared to most people's standards. It's more that the fire she's known for is gone. The feistiness is absent. The doggedness with which she reels in opponents point by point, set by set, is barely a flicker when normally, it's a roaring wildfire during a match.

She needs that fire back and clearly Kellen is struggling with how to light it. Her dad certainly knew how to.

We're in a quick break between sets, and Stevie is already down two. A few celebrities are auctioning items off, entertaining the crowd to draw this whole experience out, and I'm here, struggling to know how to get my client back on track.

"How do I fucking fix this?" she shouts to no one and everyone in the room.

"Greshenko is an ass and everyone knows it. You'll come out looking good regardless if you win or you lose," Kellen says, trying to find a way to comfort her and calm her down.

"Look good or look like the poor victim who lost her dad? I don't need a pity party, Kell, and I sure as fuck refuse to look like the victim."

He opens his mouth and then shuts it. *Smart man.*

"Isn't that the look you were going for?" I ask, clearly not as smart as Kellen and not giving a flying fuck either. My job isn't to coddle her. It's to push her and make her better. To make her see through the bullshit and get back to being at the top of her game where she normally deserves to be.

"Fuck you, Finn. No one asked you to be here," she says, turning her animus on me.

I know her words are empty and she's taking out her frustration on me—she won't be the first athlete and definitely won't be the last either— so I take them with a grain of salt.

"You only have yourself to blame." My nonchalant shrug is to push her just as hard as my words do. To try and spark that fire in her.

"Get him out of here," she says, pointing to the door, but neither

Kellen nor her bodyguards stationed at the door move. Apparently, they're sick of her bullshit too.

I'm just super competitive and refuse to lose.

Her words come back and hit my ears. Words that I'm suddenly trying to figure out how to use in my favor to spur her on.

"Get. Out." Her eyes meet mine for the first time. There is desperation, anger, and frustration all mixed in them, but the one that affects me the most is the one that looks like a lost little girl trying to find her way.

I don't have time to process that look or acknowledge the shit it stirs inside of me. I'm not here to play psychologist. I'm here to make her look like Stevie fucking Lancaster on the world stage, which is being broadcast across the globe. The stage that she needs to shine on instead of briefly sparkling on.

I'm just super competitive and refuse to lose.

"Double or nothing," I blurt out, my mouth working faster than my brain as I try to figure out how this could work.

"What?" Both her and Kellen narrow their eyes at me.

"Go back out there and challenge Greshenko on the court to double or nothing. Make a big deal of it. Grab a microphone and play it up to the crowd. Joke and tell him that he's so sure he's going to win he'll have no problem agreeing."

Stevie stares at me with her face flushed red from exertion, eyes widening while she tries to figure out what I'm getting at.

I continue. "Tell him if he wins, you'll donate your portion of earnings that you're receiving from this exhibition to Net Gen and if you win he'll have to do the same. The crowd will go nuts and it will liven them up too."

"Are you crazy?" She turns to face me, her hands on her hips, her eyes alive. "Do you know how much money you're talking about? Do you—"

"I'm well aware of the figure," I say. It's a rather large one. "And that's why he'll take the bet because he's Ian and only wants to look good for himself. He'll think he's safe and when he finishes the game in one more set it'll only be a further insult to you."

"Exactly. When *he* wins the next set." She snorts but there's a flicker there in her eyes. There's anger as a result of my words.

"Then when you kick his ass, you'll look like a hero."

"You realize I'd have to win three straight sets, right?" She rubs a towel over her face almost as if she's dismissing me.

"I'm aware."

"Against Ian Greshenko."

"*And?*"

"You don't see this as obscene?" she asks, her voice rising in pitch.

"Not in the least."

"Do you not see how I'm playing out there?"

"Then play better." I add a little fuel to her fire.

"Says the man who's sitting on the sidelines."

"Says the man telling you that you can beat him."

Stevie snorts, braces her hand on the back of the chair in front of her, and lets her head hang down as she chuckles. Kellen steps back, clearly wanting out of this conversation. I'm assuming it's to avoid the fallout if I'm wrong . . . but at the same time, he should be pushing her just the same.

I'll need to have a talk with him. He's the one who's contributing to her doubt right now by being too careful with her. Her dad wouldn't have handled her with kid gloves. Hell, everyone who follows tennis knows that. Instead he made her tough, feisty, strong. *She needs that.* To be pushed. Questioned. Challenged.

And Kellen needs to foster that.

"You're crazy," she murmurs.

"Don't you believe in yourself anymore, Stevie? Because I do."

"I believe in the old Stevie."

"Well you better start believing in the fucking new one right this minute," I shout at her.

"This one, right here, hasn't trained hard enough to trust her." Her voice is all but a whisper when she speaks and lifts her eyes to meet mine. And fucking hell, that haunted look is in her eyes again, and I look away to avoid it. I pace from one side of the room and back, running a hand through my hair and sighing in frustration as I do.

"Fine. Do what you want. No skin off my back. But the old Stevie you still believe in would never lie down and die for a prick like Greshenko. *Never.*"

And with that, I waltz out of the locker room and back to my seats in her box next to the court, hoping the ember I just sparked turns into fire.

Hoping that it burns so bright it consumes her so she forgets everything else and just plays the game *her* way.

The one I think she loves more than anything in the world.

Let's hope I'm right.

The crowd roars as Stevie hits a backhand that flies to just inside the fault line—less than an inch out of reach of Ian's racket.

She pumps her fist and shouts, clearly feeding off their energy.

She did just what I told her to do.

She walked out of that locker room and taunted Ian. She pulled the crowd into the bet, getting them to cheer for him to agree to it, so that he had no choice but to say yes on national television or look like he didn't want to support Net Gen . . . and then somehow, someway, Stevie turned it on.

She turned it on and hasn't looked back since, winning two straight sets in a row and dominating the match in a way that even has me caught up in it.

It's not only me pulling for her now though. The crowd has turned in her favor, the underdog always a favorite. And when I take a quick peek on social media during a water break, the negative comments have turned to support. The jeers to cheers.

Despite the shaky start, Stevie stands with her hands on her hips beneath the blinding lights of the court.

"Nice serve," she says with a chuckle after Greshenko serves an ace. "But you know I simply gave that to you. I wouldn't want you to have a bruised ego from me both winning the match and having more aces." Her smile is taunting as she all but curtsies at him, egging him on.

The crowd chuckles as Ian's grumble comes off less than sincere.

I hate to admit it, but the woman is phenomenal.

Sure, she may be a mess and be stubborn as hell, and I still might be grumbling that I'm her fucking babysitter, but the decision rests a little easier tonight after what I just witnessed. A woman clearly lost in whoever she is (unless of course, she's arguing with me) and who was losing by an embarrassing margin, pulled herself together to be who everyone expected her to be. That's not an easy task by any means. It's admirable in so many senses of the word, and I sit here looking at her in a slightly different light.

Simply put, what she just did was exceptional. There's no other word to describe it.

She went from what looked to me like a breakdown during the first two sets she lost, and then in the locker room during the intermission, to having complete command of the court. Her comments to the crowd are witty and her athletic prowess is remarkable.

For the first time, I see glimpses of the woman she might have been before her father's death and am impressed.

The crowd cheers as Stevie returns Ian's serve, forcing the game to a break point, the chance she's made for herself to gain a set point during Ian's serve.

Ian's livid. He paces back and forth behind the fault line, fixing the strings in his racket as he mumbles to himself, looking like a madman while Stevie waits patiently.

"Break point," the chair umpire murmurs and the crowd quiets.

Ian serves, and Stevie returns the tennis ball with a powerful backhand followed a split second later by a grunt that echoes through the stadium. The ball lands just out of reach of his racket and the crowd erupts in cheers.

And she continues on.

To win points.

Then games.

Then sets.

And then she sits in the fifth set, the sixth game with a score of forty to love. The crowd hums with anticipation as they all stand on their feet to watch the number-one ranked man in tennis be beaten by a woman.

She serves with her signature grunt following. Ian returns the serve. The ball hits the top part of the net before falling back onto his side.

The crowd goes crazy. People are cheering and screaming as the biggest grin owns Stevie's lips. She tilts her head up to the sky with her eyes closed for the briefest of seconds. It's almost as if she needs to take this all in—or as if she's talking to her dad on the stage he set up for her to succeed on.

Either way, I already know this image will be the one blasted all over the media and it couldn't be a better one. This tennis sweetheart is back and looking damn good.

I move toward the locker room as the pomp and circumstance continues on the court and shake hands with some people I know on the way. This is Stevie's time to shine, and I can only hope she takes what happened here tonight and uses it as motivation to stay on this track. To be done with her wild streak or whatever the hell she was doing.

My phone vibrates in my pocket. I know without even looking at the screen that it's Carson calling, wanting to know what the hell turned things around tonight.

I'll gladly take the credit, but it was all her. *All Stevie.*

I let the phone ring and will call him back once I get inside the locker room and away from all this noise.

There's a tug on my arm and I turn, surprised to find Stevie with her wild eyes and magnetic smile standing before me. She should be soaking up the moment.

"Finn." She says my name and doesn't even give me time to respond before she launches herself into my arms in a huge bear hug.

Taken aback, I think I chuckle, I think I say her name, but I *know* I wrap my arms around her and hug her too.

"Congratulations," I murmur into her ear, completely unaware if she can hear me above the noise of the crowd. "I knew you could do it."

I'm not sure why I say those words, but I realize the minute they're out of my mouth that I truly mean them. For some reason, I knew she could beat Ian.

Stevie leans back with tears glistening in her eyes and her arms still holding tight around me and smiles softly.

"I—thank you."

And there's that look again from her. The one that screams she's still a lost little girl—that maybe only I can see for some reason.

But this time I can't shake away how it makes me feel because she's in my arms and her lips are inches from mine, and Jesus Christ, there are a million people around us but all I can think about is her lips.

In wanting to kiss her.

Fucking hell.

I can't be thinking about shit like this right now. About how much I want her. About how fucking hard it is to keep her at a distance when I have to deal with her moment by moment.

My cold shoulder was working perfectly to keep her at a distance— to keep this from happening—until right now. Until she was in my arms, her lips close to mine, her body pressed to me, and adrenaline pumping through both of our bodies.

We stand in this extended state of anticipation, staring at each other without speaking for a few long seconds, before the noise of the crowd seeps in and the flash of the cameras break through my focus.

Stevie and I jolt away from each other as if we've been electrocuted.

What the fuck just happened?

Chapter
SIXTEEN

Stevie

I'M AMPED, RESTLESS, AND STUCK IN THAT STATE BETWEEN UTTER exhaustion and wanting to ride the high of tonight.

"You only have a few more interviews," Hayley says when she walks into what we're using as a green room between media interviews. "Then you're done."

"Thank God," I say, leaning back against the couch and closing my eyes. For a moment, I relive tonight's match. The grimace on Greshenko's face when he realized he couldn't salvage the match. The roar of the crowd when I won. The look in Finn's eyes as he stared at me.

Hayley stands just inside the door with her back to the wall, eyeing me. I don't exactly like her—or rather I haven't exactly been easy on her during her short tenure—so I'm sure she's waiting for a temper tantrum of some sort from me.

I'm too tired and at the same time too damn relieved to do any of the above.

"I want to prepare you though—"

"I can handle the questions about my dad. I'll be fine." I wave a hand at her. It's not like I haven't been answering them all night long anyway.

Of course, it affected me stepping onto the court without him sitting in the stands, his red hat the beacon I'd look to when I was struggling.

"That's not what I was going to say." Her smile is tight, her hands fidgeting. "ESPN just ran a story."

"As they should." I snicker. "I beat the number one men's seed. It's a big friggin' deal."

"Look it up on your phone," she states and there's something about her tone or the pinched expression on her face that grabs my attention.

I groan as I pick up my phone on the couch next to me. *What is it now? What are they going to dredge up to try and minimize this accomplishment?* Because it's not as if some of the journalists tonight haven't already tried to rewrite the fact that I beat Ian—downplay that a woman beat a man—by implying that he went easier on me after the intermission when I turned it around.

The accusation is total bullshit and they know it.

So I wait for the story to load with my hackles already raised and my temper ready to fire.

And then the cover picture loads, and I'm not exactly sure what to think or say or how to even feel at the image looking back at me.

It's not of me on the court after I won like I would have expected, where I was looking up at the sky with my eyes closed talking silently to my dad. The picture of victory with a cost.

Nope. Not in the least.

Instead, it's of when I ran to Finn after the match, needing to thank him somehow for believing in me when even I didn't. For egging me on so I didn't give up and make an ass out of myself on national television. For having the guts to say what he said when I've been nothing but a bitch to him over the past week.

The image is when I'm in Finn's arms and we're looking at each other, our faces inches apart.

To anyone on the outside who doesn't know our history, it looks like we're gazing lovingly at each other. A couple celebrating victory.

Knowing our history—the banter, the fighting, the being stuck together—I'm not exactly sure how to feel about the portrayal or implication.

I know I hate that my throat feels like it's closing up as I study the two of us. As I take in his dark eyes and smile that is equal parts pride and happiness. As I study the way he's looking at me—as if there is more there than an angry agent forced to be with a punk client.

His look stirs things inside of me that I'm not sure I want stirred. Lust is fine. Using sex to feel in sensations is all that I was looking for originally when it came to him.

But looking at this photo, looking at the way we're staring at each other, a part of me wants him to look at me like that all the time rather than just in a snapshot of time.

I shake my head to clear the stupid thought and try to remember the many reasons I'm supposed to hate him. The problem with that train of thought is after tonight, after he believed in me when I didn't even believe in myself, it's a lot harder to shake them than it was before.

"Did you read the article?" Hayley asks.

I scroll down and grit my teeth when I see the words to the story. "New relationship." "Love interest calms Lancaster." "A calming force to the hurricane." "Who is Stevie's new man?" "Is Finn Sanderson the one who made the difference?"

"Jesus Christ," I mutter.

"At least it takes the spotlight off your other . . . ventures of late."

I snort in disgust and she startles. "Yeah, but it implies that he's the reason I won. That I need a man at my back—or in their eyes *leading me*—to succeed. Fucking pricks."

"We can respond with something similar, *minus* the fucking pricks part, if you'd like," she says.

"Yeah. Sure," I murmur, glancing back at my phone and getting lost in the picture again.

My eyes go blurry and I sniff the tears away as I stare at the two of us. A man more than sure of himself and a woman who didn't realize until just now, how lonely she is.

That's what that was. The running over to him. The hugging him. The trying to tell him without words how much his belief in me meant.

It was the fact that after every match, I'd always shake my opponent's hand over the net and then go hug my dad.

Always.

And tonight, when I played the first real match since his passing—when I won—I was a little lost with where to go and what to do. As much as I resent and respect my dad in equal measure, he was still my best friend.

With him gone, I've lost my harshest critic, my biggest believer, and my closest friend.

Chapter
SEVENTEEN

Stevie

"WHAT THE HELL HAPPENED LAST NIGHT?" CARSON ASKS.

"I won," I say into my cell with a glance toward the closed door of Finn's room in the suite. The same door I looked at last night when I came back after the press junket, wanting to talk to him, to explain away the hug and the crazy rumors he was going to wake up to, but figuring I better leave well enough alone.

Does he know yet that the world thinks we're a couple?

God help me when he does. I mean, if the man rejects my kiss, he's going to hate the world thinking we do so much more.

"That's not what I'm talking about," he grits out, and I suddenly stiffen when I realize what I thought was excitement in his voice actually sounds like anger.

Jesus. What now? Can't I do *anything* fucking right?

"I don't understand, Carson. I thought—"

"After all that . . . and then you. Then he . . ." He says something that sounds like a curse. "I deserve answers."

"Well, hello to you too," I mutter as I take a seat on the edge of the couch, my muscles more than sore from last night's game. "I mean, I thought you'd be full of praise."

"I did leave praise. Check your voicemail and texts. They're all there. That's why none of this makes sense. Obviously whatever Finn was doing was working so why did you fuck it up?"

Carson cusses but not at me. He's old school and thinks women shouldn't hear profanity so, I'm a little taken aback when he throws *fuck* in there.

Besides, of all the days in the past two months, yesterday was the one day where I felt like I did everything right. And as if it doesn't matter, I'm still being accused of doing something wrong.

"Carson. Just tell me what you think I did. I'm sure there's a valid explanation I can give to—"

"*He quit.*" Emotion I can't pinpoint vibrates through Carson's voice.

"Who quit?" I ask, startling, but I'm already pushing off the couch and moving toward the closed door I was looking at moments ago.

There's no way *he'd* quit. Not after last night. Not after we actually worked together instead of apart. Not after—

"Oh." It's all I say when I push his door open to his room to find the bed made and all of his things gone. *Finn quit?*

"He called just a moment ago and told me that he will no longer be able to represent—"

"Babysit—" I whisper in some kind of reflexive reaction that doesn't even matter at this point and time.

"—you, and I want to know what the hell you did because it takes a hell of a lot to make him walk away from someone."

Finn quit . . .

"I don't understand."

"That makes two of us, Stevie. The man who was clearly helping get you back on the right side of wrong walked away and I deserve an answer as to why."

"I—I—" *I tried to kiss him. The world thinks we're a couple. He's seen me naked.* The thoughts run a marathon through my head but none of them make sense. None of them are valid reasons why he would quit. Especially after the success of last night. "I don't know. He didn't give a reason? An explanation? Anything?"

"Just that he thought he'd be able to make it work, but now doesn't think it will."

"So he quit on me." My own words sting as I say them. It didn't matter how well I did last night or that I came back and fought, he still quit on me.

He still left me.

The minute the tears well up, my temper ignites with a raging anger I don't completely understand. It's the only way I know how to cope with this type of rejection. With being abandoned yet again.

"I've got—my other line is going—Christ, kid, I *needed* him to help you."

Disappointment rings through his tone. Is his anger directed at both Finn *and* me?

I shake my head, although Carson can't see it before the call disconnects.

I stare at Finn's empty room and his bed that obviously wasn't slept in. Did he even come back here last night? Did he come back but never sleep as he pondered what to do?

I behave and this is what I get?

Confusion reigns and anger builds as I try to understand what happened. As I try to fathom why I'm so hurt by this when I didn't want him here as my shadow in the first place.

But I am hurt.

And rejected.

And questioning myself.

With the phone in my hand, I close the door and blink away the tears.

Fuck Finn Sanderson.

Fuck him and his lack of reasons.

Carson's wrong. I don't need him.

I don't need anyone.

I'm hurt when I shouldn't be.

I'm angry when I know I'm the one who put myself in this position.

But more than anything, I wonder why I wanted a man I disliked—purely because of circumstance—to still like me.

Chapter
EIGHTEEN

Finn

"SANDERSON." CARSON'S VOICE COMES THROUGH LOUD AND CLEAR on the voicemail, and I cringe. I deserve whatever shit he's going to give me. "I understand why you don't want to take on Stevie as a client, and I respect your decision. I can't say that I'm not disappointed in it, but I understand there are times in your life when certain clients aren't beneficial to you or your brand." He sighs heavily. "Whatever your reasons are, I'm sure you'll explain them to me someday. *And yes, apparently, I'm getting softer in my old age.*" His chuckle can be heard before the line goes dead.

I stare at my cell and shake my head, marveling at the man I look to as a father. He knew I've been stressing over my call to him and took the pressure off me by calling first.

He knew what I needed to hear.

I think of the years I endured verbal abuse from my own dad. The constant pushing from a man who never made much of himself so he needed me to be and do what he never could. I recall the moment, a few months after Carson took me under his wing, where I realized what a cancer my own father was in my life.

I swirl the drink in my glass and rest my arms on the bar, head angled down, and try to ignore the sickening feeling in my gut. *I definitely don't deserve Carson Vega in my life.*

I know I'm letting my mentor down, but he's letting me down as well. At least that was the double whammy gut punch I felt when I got the phone call late last night as I headed back to the suite after the match.

I'll find a way to make this up to him.

I know I will.

Chapter
NINETEEN

Finn

"Fucking Finn. Always stealing the pretty girls."

"It's a bullshit story meant to sell headlines," I mutter. The image of Stevie staring at me is now burned into my memory. The image all over social media I simultaneously wanted to tear my eyes from and couldn't stop staring at.

The problem is I'm not sure why.

"Story or not," my close friend and NFL pro-bowler, Gabe, says, "she was in your arms looking at you all lovey, dovey."

"I'm her fucking babysitter is what I am."

He snorts. "So you're into the kinky role-playing then? Does she wear the schoolgirl uniform when she comes over so you have to bend her over your knee and spank her into submission?" His laugh fills the line.

"Fuck you."

We banter like this. It's what we do.

So I'm not sure why it bugs me this time.

"Oh." His laughter stops as he feels out whether the words are playful or serious. "So the look was genuine, then?"

"What look?" I stop outside the entrance to the casino. On one side of me, there's a half-dressed woman walking around in stripper heels trying to sell photos with her and on the other, a man dressed up like Michael Jackson, busking for money. I don't pay attention to either because I'm so focused on Gabe.

"The one the whole world saw tonight. The look that says Carson is right."

"Come again?"

"Well, isn't he how the two of you connected? I thought he stepped in to rep her and then all of a sudden I see that you're there, so I assumed—"

"He handed her off to me. That's right. What exactly did you mean about Carson being right though?" I hold my finger to my open ear and try to find a stretch of somewhat quiet so I can hear what he's saying.

"Clearly you've been working too much and haven't been paying attention to the life that's all around you."

"Gabe, get to the fucking point." I'm tired and want to know what the hell he's talking about.

"Did you see that Tori Belcher and Ronnie Feldman are engaged?" he asks out of the blue about the WSL soccer player and MLB pitcher.

"Yeah, I sent them a congratulations message. What does that have to do with me?"

"What about Tommy Tuttle and Simone Grandy?" An NFL pro-bowler and an Olympic gymnast. "They were married last year."

"Gabe," I warn.

"Do you know what they all have in common?" My sigh is my only response. "They met after Carson—wink, wink—pushed them together through some project."

"Uh-huh." I roll my eyes and give a shake of my head he can't see.

"I'm serious. He's getting sentimental in his old age and keeps giving everyone the speech about finding someone to enjoy life with as he's shoving them together," he says as I dig in my pocket and put some money in a panhandler's cup.

Carson knows me better than that. He knows how I am, how I—

"How was it the two of you came to work together again?" Sarcasm drips from his words.

"It doesn't matter how we came to work together." I sigh. "It matters that there's nothing between us."

"You're such a fucking liar, Sanderson. You think I'm buying that shit when the evidence is there in full fucking color?" He laughs and I groan.

"Whatever." I shove a hand in my pocket and decide to walk around to another entrance to the casino to buy time.

"Whatever? I think the evidence is in the fact you haven't hit that yet."

"*Meaning?*"

"*Meaning once you fuck a chick, you move on. The only woman you didn't do that to was Chase Kincade, and you played cat and mouse with her for months before you dated her for a while.*"

He's right. I don't want to admit it so I keep my mouth fucking shut.

I pursued Chase for way too long. I like to think it was the hard-to-get thing that fueled me on when normally I would have dropped interest, but it was more than that.

I liked Chase. I liked her a lot. She wasn't a fall-at-your-feet type of girl. They're a dime a dozen these days. Instead, she was combative, independent, determined, feisty, and told me how it was.

Kind of like Stevie is.

I push the thought out of my head just as quickly as it drifts in. Chase is nothing like Stevie. Not in the least.

Besides, when push came to shove and shit got too serious, I cheated on Chase. Cheated on her with a random chick because it was so much easier to have her make the call and dump me.

So much easier than admitting I was freaked the fuck out that I liked her more than I admitted and was waiting for the other shoe to drop. That I was waiting for her to leave me like it had been ingrained in me my whole life.

"*Let's get something straight, here, Stevie isn't Chase. I'm temporarily in charge of getting Stevie's career back on track. The last thing I need to do is sleep with her.*"

"*I think that's exactly what you need to do.*"

"*We . . . never mind.*" *My hesitation says it all and fucking hell.*

"*Oooooh,*" *Gabe shouts into the phone.* "*That means you want to then.*"

"*All I was going to say is that we have a professional relationship but I figured it wouldn't do any good to say it.*"

"*I have a professional relationship with my agent too, but I don't look at her like you looked at Stevie tonight.*"

Fuck.

Just fuck.

"*You're being an asshole,*" *I mutter.*

"*Yep, just like you always are to me. Jesus, man. She's really got you all* twisted up," he says and I admit nothing because there's nothing to admit. "Nothing says Finn Sanderson is done with a woman like him admitting he slept with her. So fuck her, already. Get her out of your system so you can move on. She'll hate you for it, but it will make working with her that much easier."

"Spoken by a man who clearly has a superior moral compass." I enter the casino and am assaulted by the unmistakable scents of Vegas. "Aren't you the same man who thought it was a wise move to date your quarterback's ex-wife?" When he doesn't answer, I say, "Yeah, that's what I thought."

"Touché, my friend. Touché." He chuckles as I make my way to the elevator in this maze of a casino. "When do I get to see you again?"

"When I'm done with this babysitting job. I think I'm going to work from the West Coast for a while—"

"Your house in San Diego?" he asks, his voice excited. We had way too much fun—er trouble—the last time he visited.

"I think. I'll let you know."

"Sounds good. Hey, Finn?"

"Hmm?" I enter the elevator.

"Do me a favor. Thank Carson for the matchmaking service, then fuck her and get her out of your system. This much confusion isn't healthy for a man."

"Yeah, yeah," I mutter as he hangs up and I'm left walking down the hallway of the hotel, thinking about shit I never thought I'd be thinking about when I woke up this morning.

Like if Carson set this up like it's a dating game.

Like why I walked away from Stevie when she tried to kiss me, and it has nothing to do with me being her agent and needing to stay professional.

Like why right now all I keep thinking about is the expression on my face in that viral image. I'm not sure how I feel about it.

The problem is whether Carson set up this whole thing or not, it fucking worked.

I'm the one entering the suite and staring at her closed door, wondering if she's in there and wanting to see her. I'm the one thinking way too much about almost kisses and missed opportunities that first night.

Then again, if I listen to Gabe, if I had slept with her that first night, none of this would even be crossing my mind.

I'd have washed my hands of her in that aspect and moved on. Well at least I moved on.

And kissed goodbye a six-figure package.

"Rough day, sugar?"

I startle from my thoughts about my earlier phone call with Gabe, glance over, and smile politely at the waitress as she cleans empty glasses and bottles off her tray. Her smile is soft and her eyes are kind—a total contrast to the ridiculous feather and jewel outfit the casino makes her wear that fits in with their motif.

"Something like that," I murmur and take a sip, replaying last night and my phone call to Carson earlier through my head.

You're disappointing me, son.

"It's slow. I've got time if you need an ear."

She must think I'm pathetic, sitting here drinking whiskey by myself in the middle of the day as if I were a gambling addict after a rough night of losses.

There's a cheer that goes up from the other side of the casino and I glance that way before answering. "Thanks. I appreciate the offer, but I'm good."

I was counting on you to help me out and last night was proof that you were the right person for the job.

"Okay. Should I get you another one then?" She tips her head to my half-empty glass.

"Nah. I have client meetings I need to get to. Phone calls." It's not a lie, but the last thing I want to do right now is work. "I should get up to my room."

"Okay. Well, best of luck with them." Another round of yelling goes up and she stands on her tippy-toes to look and see but shrugs as if she can't see anything.

"At least someone's getting lucky," I murmur.

She laughs and pats me on the shoulder. "I hope whoever she is, she's worth this misery you seem to have found yourself in."

My smile falters. "Excuse me?"

"I've been doing this for over ten years. I know a man in misery over a woman when I see one and you, sir, are the perfect picture of just that."

I open my mouth to refute her but leave it be.

It doesn't matter to her.

But hell if it doesn't matter to me. I slide some tip money across the bar with the intention of heading up to the new room I booked last night. The one that gave me a little more space from *her* so that I could clear my head and prepare to call Carson.

The call I made but the confrontation I didn't have. Why didn't I ask him if Gabe was right and that he set this all up?

Isn't that the question of the fucking day?

Is it because I was afraid the answer would be yes or because regardless of the answer, there's an undeniable attraction and chemistry between us?

Even now, I'm fucking thinking about her.

"I just don't think we gel well, Carson. Last night was a fluke and she pulled it off, but I'm not the right fit for her."

Right fit for her my ass.

But it was my excuse. My reasoning.

And it's a damn good one to smother how I feel about last night. The look on her face. The one captured by the camera and spread around the world.

Stevie is falling for me, and I can't have that.

I quit because of her.

Not because of how I feel at all.

"Thanks." I smile and rise from my seat, drink still in hand, as a chant breaks out that I can't quite make out.

Of course, I look.

Anything to take my mind off my current misery and avoidance is clearly welcome. And lucky for me, the crowd chanting in a circle is in the direction I'm headed.

But it's only when I get closer that I notice it's mostly men stretching on their toes and craning to see, with phones held above their heads to record whatever's happening.

It's only then that I catch on to the chant.

Ste-vie!

Ste-vie!

I catch a glimpse on one of the phone screens being held up. I know that head of blond hair.

Oh. Shit.

Chapter

TWENTY

Stevie

THE SHOTS OF TEQUILA ARE LINED UP ON THE EDGE OF THE POKER table. Four are empty and six are sitting there waiting for me to fail.

"Stevie." I hear my name, an angry sound against all the encouraging ones. "Goddammit, Lancaster."

The crowd around me parts as I wiggle my bra out through the armhole of my shirt and fling it onto the poker table, the black lace a contrast to the green felt. I should be worried about what item of clothing I'll have to remove next time I lose a hand, but I'm not. I'm more focused on the tequila that will taste like acid as it goes down.

But not drinking it means I feel. And I don't want to feel. I want to drink another shot to help push me back into the numbing abyss I've been living in.

I grit my teeth when Finn breaks through the crowd—the owner of the voice—and meet his eyes as I down another shot.

The crowd around me cheers while I stare at him, a *fuck you* lift to my eyebrow as I turn back to the dealer and smile. "Shall we?"

I don't know shit about poker—how to play, the terms, what to do—but I know the rules of this bet were when one player loses a hand, they have to remove an item of clothing and take a shot.

Needless to say, the man across from me is fully clothed and I'm sitting without shoes, socks, and now my bra.

"Stevie. Let's go," Finn demands as he pushes his way through the crowd toward me.

"Leave her the hell alone, man," comes from the right. The voice's owner, a big, burly guy, stops Finn's progress.

"I'm fine. I'm good." My head swims with the tequila, and I wave a hand at Finn as the dealer deals the cards. I close my eyes for a quick second, and then try to focus on the cards without lifting them too high. I don't want to meet the pair of eyes across the table from me.

The asshole who badgered me as I walked through the casino. Telling me how last night had to have been rigged because there's no way I beat Ian Greshenko without it being fixed. The prick who got in my face and told me I wasn't good enough to have won. *I hate men. I truly hate them all.*

And then I exploded. A dare from him, a challenge from me one-upping the stakes, and here we are—strip poker on the floor of a Vegas casino.

Vivi and Jordan would be proud that I created my own Cards O' Fun without them.

Besides, *this*—the alcohol, the challenge, the adrenaline pumping through me—is what I needed to feel like me again after the blow I got this morning from Carson about Finn.

"Stevie. This isn't what you need—"

"You gave up the right to know what I need or don't need when you quit on me." I shout the words at him across the table, not really caring who hears or how it makes him feel.

"Your boyfriend coming to save you from the embarrassment? Pretty little princess needs rescuing?" my opponent, Hank, asks from his spot across the table with a smug grin.

"He's nothing to me," I mutter as I glance at the cards in my hand and the two sitting face up on the table in front of me. I have a shit hand. No pairs. No straights. No flushes. With a measured breath to not show my hand, I push two, one-hundred-dollar chips into the pot and hope I can bluff my way into not having to remove another item of clothing before the last card is turned over.

"Two hundred?" Hank lifts an eyebrow and glances over to Finn, who is making a scene I don't want right now. Ha. I guess I'm making a scene too, but what do I care. That's par for the course with me. I wonder if Finn would appreciate a lecture about how to act in public. About how you need to be on your best behavior since it's not easy to repair a damaged reputation. "That's all?" Hank taunts. "Must not have a good hand."

"I believe I've already put one thousand in the pot. Think what you want to think, but you're the one who's getting close to losing his pants." I lean back and smile at him, praying for at least a pair of Kings with the river card.

"I think you're bluffing." He matches my ante and the dealer turns the river card over. Hank fist-pumps with a shout while I cringe.

I've got a big fat nothing. The crowd around us doesn't know it and starts chanting my name again for me to turn over my cards.

Either that or for me to remove another item of clothing.

I take the shot of tequila before I turn over the cards and the crowd roars when they see I have nothing to beat Hank.

"A bet's a bet," I say, swaying a little when I stand, my hands going to the button of my denim shorts.

"Party's over." It's the last words I hear before Finn's hands are pushing my hands off my waist and forcing me back from the table.

I shove him but he doesn't budge an inch. "I'm not your problem anymore," I grit at him as I reach for another shot that he slaps my hand away from.

"Christ, woman." It's a swear below the hum of people shouting at him to leave me alone, but he doesn't care. He doesn't even flinch when I push his shoulder as he simultaneously grabs my bra and remaining chips off the poker table before trying to escort me out of there.

Fury courses through my veins. "Leave me alone. You don't get to tell me—"

"Like hell I don't," Finn says before picking me up and throwing me over his shoulder like I'm a sack of potatoes who doesn't have a say.

"Put. Me. Down," I shout, my legs kicking and my hands slapping at his butt as he tightens his grip over my thighs while walking through the casino like nothing is amiss.

People are staring.

At least I assume they are because I'm face down being treated like a little kid, but not a single person steps in to help me out. Instead, I see flashes from phones taking pictures.

By now, not only is my head dizzy but I'm panting from trying to wriggle out of his grasp.

"I swear to God, Finn," I say as the elevator dings and he strides into it and closes the doors, telling other people they can't get on. "Put me down."

But he doesn't. He just adjusts me on his shoulder and tightens his grip. "How the ever-loving fuck does one even get into a strip poker game on the floor of a casino, huh? How does that even happen?"

"It's pretty easy when you're Stevie Lancaster," I snipe back.

"You know what's even easier? Having a million videos and pictures of you all over the Internet, half dressed and totally drunk."

"Well, it sure as shit beats the picture of you and me from last night being everywhere." My words smother the small space and Finn doesn't respond.

Where the alcohol was numbing before, now it's just pure, unfettered anger. Sobering and almost invigorating.

The elevator dings.

He strides with me down the hall and only after he enters my suite with the key card he must have kept, does he put me down. And by put me down, I mean he throws me on the bed before walking back out as if he didn't just haul me up here like he owned me.

I'm up and scrambling to go after him within a second.

"Who the hell do you think you are?" I scream, picking up the throw pillow on the couch as I walk past it and throw at his back.

It hits him squarely between the shoulder blades and he turns back on me so quickly that it knocks me off my stride.

"Who the hell do I think *I am*? I'm the man who just saved your ass from causing a scene that you wouldn't be able to undo." He steps into me, the muscle in his jaw ticking and the tendons in his neck taut as he jabs his finger at himself as if to make the point.

"I don't want your help."

"I'm sure you don't through your drunken goddamn haze but rest assured, you needed it."

"I didn't. Especially not from a quitter like you."

And there it is—the reason I'm angrier than anything—laid out between us.

He quit on me when I thought he believed in me.

He quit on me when, compared to the loneliness of the last few horrific months, I finally had someone to anchor me.

He quit on me when he made me want him even though I didn't want to.

"A quitter like me?" His eyes narrow as he steps even closer. His voice is calm and even where mine is wild and crazy. I don't care because he hurt me when I'm so sick of being hurt. "I thought that was exactly what you wanted, Stevie. For me to quit so you could go crazy and sabotage the rest of your career to the best of your ability." He hooks a thumb over his shoulder toward the door. "Case in point, downstairs."

"Case in point? How about case in point that you're not the man I thought you were?"

"Oh, I'm wounded. As if you had me figured out in the whole ten days I've known you."

"I have you figured out a whole lot more than you think I do." I push against his chest, begging for a reaction from him. Needing him to feel as out of control as I feel right now. "I just didn't figure you for a pussy who ran away when shit got real."

"A pussy?" he scoffs.

"You're goddamn right, a pussy. Get a little spooked that God forbid the world thinks you're dating me? I'm sorry that the prospect is so bad you have to quit." My voice breaks on the last words and I hate myself for it.

Screw this.

Screw him.

"I hate you," I grit out and push against his chest, but this time he grabs my wrists with an iron-like grip.

"I'm not real thrilled with you either." His eyes lock on mine and I can feel his heartbeat against my hand.

"You're a bully."

I hate you.

I want you.

Why does it have to be you?

"And you're a rebel."

"Well, aren't we quite the pair," I murmur, the anger suddenly ebbing as desire fights its way to the surface.

Our eyes lock. My breath hitches as he exhales oh, so slowly.

And then from one beat to the next, his lips are on mine. The kiss is hungry and angry and frustrated and ravenous all at the same time, if that's even possible.

It's like we're fighting without words, each of us needing more from the other and taking it with scrapes of teeth and licks of tongues.

"I don't like you like the article suggests I do," he grates out before fisting his hand in my hair and forcing my head to tilt up.

"Good. Great. Neither do I," I say, the last word coming out as a moan.

"This is just sex." His free hand cups my ass and presses me against him.

"Just sex," I repeat before his mouth meets mine again in another soul-emptying kiss that leaves my body aching for more and my head swimming with the sudden shift in gears.

His hands. They feel like heaven as they roam over my body with an angst and demand that tells me he's battling the same battle I am—desperation meshed with anger.

His kisses. They're greed tinged with need woven with hunger.

His groans. So guttural, as his hands map my body and find their way inside my shorts to push them down. An aural seduction.

His cock. Jesus. Can he just put it in me already?

"Finn," I moan, needing more, wanting more, despite being furious at him.

His teeth scrape over my shoulder as he unbuckles his pants and shoves them down to his ankles.

There is no time to remove shoes, no need to take shirts off.

The only thing that matters is the end game. The climax after the rise. The blissful fall after the ravenous fury.

"Hurry," I urge as his hand finds its way between my thighs.

"Christ, woman," he groans and walks us backward where he swipes whatever is on the table off with his hand before pushing my ass against its edge.

His mouth is on mine again. Bruising and sensual and fraught with necessity as he pulls a condom out and protects us.

My core burns with an ache that I fear only he can put out. With a want that has been simmering since that first night we met. With a desire that's so intense, it's scary.

"Please. Finn." I arch my back and spread my legs, willing him to step in between. Begging him to.

But his fist is in my hair again as he leans over, the crest of his cock pressing at my entrance.

His lips kiss my shoulder, along the curve of my neck, up to my ear.

"For the record," he growls. "I wasn't quitting on you. I was saving you from me."

And with that, he pushes into me. Every nerve of mine sings with pleasure at the fullness of him and the sensations it evokes.

I fist my hand in the neck of his shirt and yank his face toward mine. "I don't need to be saved." I steal a kiss to quiet his response in a need to understand his words but only end up confusing matters more. "I just need to feel." I release him and lie back on the table, eyes locked on his. "Make me feel, Finn."

There's a moment where he stares at me, where something more than lust is in his eyes but it's too much to process, too much to figure out as I wait for him to punish me in the most pleasurable of ways.

The moment breaks when he slides out ever so slowly, the head of his cock teasing me, while his fingers flutter over my clit.

The sensation is torture.

It's pleasure.

It's frustrating.

It's all-consuming.

Exactly how this relationship between Finn and me has been since day one.

And then he drives back into me. But this time he doesn't stop. This time the anger is back—and the greed and the lust. This time it's hands grasping and the table moving and the sound of us connecting.

It's his thrust and my moan.

It's the lift of my hips and his groan.

It's quick and it's dirty and lacking all niceties—just how I want it. Just how I need it.

It's a shout on my lips as the wave of pleasure pins me beneath its current and drowns me in its bliss.

It's a growl of my name as his fingers dig into the flesh at my hips and hold me still when he finds his own release.

And then there's silence. Or rather the room around us is silent but for our panted breaths, and the thunder of my pulse, fills my ears as my heart decelerates and we come back to our senses.

To the knowledge that this didn't fix a goddamn thing. He still quit and I'm still livid with him for it. But the rejection stings a little less now.

I wasn't quitting on you. I was saving you from me.

Luckily, Finn pulls out of me and heads to the bathroom with only the sound of his belt where his pants are still wrapped around his ankles clinking with each step. It gives me a second to process everything. To sit up and pull my shorts back on so that we can face whatever the hell just happened fully clothed and without any evidence of sex present.

Like that's going to work since the smell of it hangs in the suite around me.

I'm just finishing buttoning my shorts when his voice is behind me. "You mind telling me how exactly you got into a strip poker, tequila-shot drinking game of Texas Hold 'Em in the middle of a casino floor?" he asks.

"It's none of your business." And I'm not sure why my first words after he just made the earth shift beneath my feet are snippy, but they are. Maybe because I already know what's going to happen next, and even though it's exactly what I want to happen—him leaving with us still at odds—I'm already preparing myself for the sting.

He snorts in reaction as if he expects nothing less in an answer than that. "Good to know everything's still the same."

"Sure is." My hands are on my hips as I study his face and try to read what his eyes are saying. I can't and so I look away, afraid he might see too much in mine if I let him. "You were an itch. I scratched it. Thanks for that."

"At your service." He chuckles with a mock bow before taking a few steps toward the door. He stops and studies me again. Words are on his lips, but he shuts them without uttering a sound.

"Just for the record," I say as he heads toward the door, "you were good, but I still don't like you."

"Good to hear. Try to stay out of trouble, Stevie."

There's a finality to the click of the door when he shuts it, a sense that this was the closure we needed to be able to part ways.

It was how we began.

And now, it is how we ended.

If that's the case, why do I feel so unsettled listening to his footsteps as he walks down the hallway?

Chapter
TWENTY-ONE

Finn

Gabe: Did your flight get delayed out of Vegas with that fire at the airport?

Me: It was canceled.

Gabe: Still heading to SD though?"

Me: In the morning.

Gabe: So . . .

Me: So . . . what?

Gabe: Did you get her out of your system?

I laugh as I look at the text when nothing about this afternoon is funny. Leaving Stevie's suite, a delayed then canceled flight to San Diego, and now the search for another hotel room. All I want to be is out of this damn city. So, yeah, not funny.

Is she out of my system?

Isn't that the fucking question of the day?

I'll admit it was hard to not go back up to her suite for another round before I left the hotel . . . to *make sure* I got her out of my system.

Hell, I even hesitated when I closed the door to her suite before I walked away, the image of her standing there in her jean shorts and a red shirt with her hardened nipples showing through the fabric burned into my mind.

Just like the look on her face is.

The look that was so contradictory to the words she spoke. Haughty, arrogant comments while her expressive eyes read confused vulnerability.

I hated the way they made me feel. I wanted to stay and make sure she was okay.

That's why I need to get out of this city, cut ties with a woman— er, client—who was never supposed to be on my radar in the first place.

Fucking Carson. I sigh and close my eyes as I sit in the back of the Uber on the way to The Strip, trying to figure out how to respond.

Me: Yeah. We're done.

Gabe: So fucking predictable, but dude, U R the man.

Me: Can't let them get too attached, now can I?

I hit send on the text and then stare at it for way too long, hating how it makes me feel.

Chapter
TWENTY-TWO

Finn

9 Years Ago

THE BAR IS CROWDED FOR A THURSDAY, BUT IT'S DOWNTOWN AND that means anything goes most nights. The music being piped in through the speakers is low and bluesy and fitting for the crowd—mid- to late-twenties, not too trendy and more urban professional. Glasses clink and talk is constant

I slide onto a seat at the bar beside my friend, Gabe, and sigh. I'm in town trailing Carson around trying to learn the ropes and even though Gabe moved on to the NFL, we still try to get together at least once a month when we can.

"It's been a long fucking week, man."

"Longest of long," he murmurs before taking a long tug on his bottle of beer before shaking his head. "Got dumped by my girl, strained my fucking groin so I'm out for a few weeks, and got rear-ended by somebody."

"You win." I hold my hands up in mock surrender. "You definitely win."

"I'd attempt to pick up the hot chick across the bar, but just my luck, she'd be a dude or have three tits or something," he mutters and then laughs, completely consumed by his own misery.

"I thought all you had to do was say you play for the NFL and chicks fall at your feet."

He looks down at the ground around us. "Just proved that theory wrong."

"Fuck off," I say around a laugh as the bartender slides my drink in front of me.

"Gladly but then you'd miss me."

"So? Which hot chick are we talking about?" I'm already looking, ready to be his wingman . . . or perhaps to fly solo and approach her myself if he's too chickenshit to do it himself.

He lifts his chin in the direction of an auburn-haired woman whose back is to us. She's svelte with curls tumbling down her back and a sophistication about her that money can't buy.

"Not bad, huh?"

"Not bad if you prefer looking at her from behind."

"The front's even better."

"Maybe she's just what you need to get over what's-her-name?" I suggest when I most definitely know his ex's name. How can I not when we may have fooled around a bit before they started dating? "How about I go be a wingman for you? See if she's single and interested?"

"The last thing I need is you to go talk to her for me. The last time you talked to a chick on my behalf you banged her like three hours later."

I laugh into my glass of whiskey and shrug. "You can't exactly blame me for being her type."

"Fucker," he mumbles playfully as I push my seat back and stand.

"I'll make up for it now," I say and give a cheesy smile.

I move around the bar, scoping out prospects for myself as I go and lean my elbow on the bar just behind the woman of interest.

"So, I have a friend," I say just above the chatter of the bar. "And he's a little nervous to come over and talk to you so I told him I'd—" And my words trail off when the woman turns to face me. She may be older now—the freckles I used to think were adorable are gone, her face slimmer and more mature, her hair definitely darker—but I'd know those eyes anywhere. "Molly?"

It takes a second for me to believe it's really her as recognition slowly etches the lines of her face.

"*Finn?* Finn Sanderson?"

She looks at me with the same disbelief I feel but I'm more than sure she doesn't experience the pang of hurt I do—*even after seven years.*

"That's me." For the first time in my life, I don't even know what to say.

"Oh my God. Hi." She grabs me in a quick hug as her laugh fills the air, and I'm not one hundred percent sure why I don't enthusiastically hug her back.

I should be over what happened. Her kiss by the gym with someone whose name I don't even remember was years—hell, a lifetime—ago and doesn't really matter in the grand scheme of things . . . but it does.

She was my first love.

My first heartbreak.

The first female who proved my dad and all his crazy nonsense about women to be true.

"Look at you!" she says, her hands on my biceps as she takes me in. "How are you? What—I mean, there are so many questions that I don't even know which one to ask first."

I have a million too, but none are as benign as *how are you?*

"I'm good," I say, glancing over to Gabe and holding my finger up to let him know to hold on a minute. The last thing I need him to think is that I'm hitting on Molly and not being a wingman, but truth be told, this whole setup just crashed and burned. "And you?"

"I am too. I'm studying for the bar exam. Corporate law." She shakes her head. "This is just so crazy seeing you again after all these years. Tell me all about you."

I'm typically a guy that isn't fazed by much. I've been slapped by dates who are pissed at me, told to go to hell by females I've dumped, trolled on social media by women who can't handle the fact that I moved on without them, but there's something about seeing her that has me back in a past I've long since left behind.

That and there's no way I'm setting her up with Gabe now. I know the irony is rich considering my long and sordid track record with women, but I don't care.

"Finn? Is something—" Her smile falls and she rolls her eyes playfully.

"You can't still be mad at me. I've forgiven you, Finn." At what must be a blank look, she continues. "I mean, what teenager wouldn't take the hundred dollars and do that?"

"Hundred?" I ask, my eyes narrowing. "What in the hell are you talking about?"

But even before the words are out, I have a sinking feeling.

"The hundred dollars your dad offered me."

My dad?

"Offered you to do what?"

Her face is a myriad of emotions as she stares at me—amusement turned to confusion, guilt meshed with time passed. "I'm sorry. Never mind I said anything." Her smile is tight and the laugh she gives is fake as fuck.

It's my hand on her bicep now. "Molly." Her name is an exhausted sigh. "What did he offer you one hundred dollars for?"

"You really don't know?" Her voice is soft, and I shake my head in response. "He told me that you were cheating on me and that you needed to be taught a lesson." She shrugs as if to try and play it off. "He offered me one hundred dollars to make out with whoever I wanted so long as I was outside the gym at a certain time."

But she was the rich girl and I was the broke boy. Her parents gave her everything she wanted . . . and yet the lure of one hundred dollars was more important to her than simply asking me for the truth.

"And you just believed him?" I ask. "You never thought to ask me? To confront me to see if—you know what?" I take a step back. "Never mind. It doesn't matter."

You don't matter.

With another shake of my head, I walk away from her feeling a million things, but two in particular stand out more than anything. My dad is definitely the bastard I know him to be—I just didn't know how much.

And . . . he was right. Women will take or do anything to screw you over.

Life lesson learned.

Take everything at face value. *Even women.*

Chapter
TWENTY-THREE

Finn

Just get me on the fucking plane.

I'm done with this city. With the smoke and the raspy-voiced waitresses who come on too strong, and the people who choose not to sleep or bathe for days in a quest to earn the almighty dollar.

I want to earn that same dollar but do it while sitting at my house on the beach and negotiating for my clients over the phone.

I want to do it away from Stevie and all the errant thoughts that she caused while sitting in my hotel room last night.

The airport crowd isn't bad for Vegas. People are dotted here and there, most sitting at the sports bar at the far end of the terminal, desperate to get one more drink, one more hand at electronic poker, one more connection, before returning to their boring, normal, everyday lives.

The news is on the TVs positioned randomly throughout the seating area. I half-heartedly watch it as I balance my coffee, my carry-on, and my backpack. My phone is vibrating inside my backpack somewhere, probably the last place I shoved it as I went through security, but I just don't have enough hands to grab it yet.

"In the sports world today," the anchor on the twenty-four-hour news station says, the opening line, always grabbing my attention. "It seems tennis superstar Stevie Lancaster just can't seem to catch her breaks. Worldwide News hasn't independently confirmed any of the source material yet, but—"

"American Airlines flight forty-four is now boarding . . ." drones over the intercom and knocks out the sound on the televisions.

But I can still see the images on the screen. Stevie leaving the Vegas hotel surrounded by press five- to six-people deep. They shove microphones in her face and shout questions at her. She lowers her head without speaking and her bodyguards help push her back into the hotel.

What the hell?

It's not your problem, Finn. Not a fucking one. Whatever she caused or is in the middle of isn't your fucking issue to deal with. And yet I stand, staring at the TV screen long after the story has moved on, unable to get the image of her standing there out of my head.

The woman is used to the media. Hell, she's lived her life under its scrutiny for most of it, but there was something about the look on her face—shell-shocked, overwhelmed, vulnerable—that says this is out of her control.

My phone vibrates again against my back, prompting me to find a seat so I can drop my shit and grab it.

It vibrates as my fingers close around it and I'm already dreading what I'm going to see on its screen. There are five missed texts from Carson as I google Stevie's name on my browser to see what the hell is going on.

After years of living in silence, Mary Johnson steps forward to speak about her tennis superstar daughter, the man who paid her off for years, and if that man, is in fact, Stevie's real father . . .

"Jesus fucking Christ," I mutter after reading the opening line of the article. I stand there, my stuff on the seat beside me, and skim the rest of the article. Cash payments made regularly to keep her away. A mother desperate to connect with her estranged daughter. A woman who was promiscuous in her early twenties who put Liam Lancaster's name on the birth certificate without knowing who Stevie's real father was.

I silence a call from Carson that comes in, needing to read this again and see what other sites say. Needing to think first before I respond to him.

Greed.

That's what this whole interview, all of these interviews that seem way too coordinated for me, screams of. They're unfounded claims from a woman desperate for attention or money.

But why now? Because Stevie's fiercest protector, Liam, is now gone? Or is there something more sinister here? An opponent trying to mess with a competitor they're fearful—or jealous—of?

I twist my lips and stare out the window to the runway and know the opponent theory is far-fetched, but I've seen it happen before.

But this? This screams a plea for money. This sounds like a desperate woman got advice from a smart person who knows Stevie is at her most vulnerable right now. That she won't want all this noise heading into training for the US Open and therefore her advisors will tell her to make the payment with a heavily clad NDA to quiet the noise so she can concentrate.

It's amazing when you're famous who comes out of the woodwork to stake their claim. And it's sad that I've seen it more times than I thought I would in my ten years of being an agent.

They announce first class boarding and I grab my stuff. This is not where I'm needed. Yes, Stevie Lancaster is going through more shit, but she has the strength and fire to beat it. *She's proven that.*

Despite the look on her face I'm trying to forget.

My phone rings again when I'm one person back from the ticket counter and I know Carson will keep calling until I answer.

"I'm boarding my flight, Car. I'll call you back when I land."

"Finn." Stevie's voice is so soft, I can barely hear her say my name.

My stomach twists at how lost she sounds.

I wait to go numb. For my ears to hear the buzz of indifference that I choose to listen to when it comes to women. For the fight or flight to kick in that always opts for flight. For my emotions to fall flat.

But they don't.

They feel.

They don't harden, they intensify.

And what the fuck is up with that?

The man in the line behind me taps my shoulder to tell me to give the airline worker my boarding pass and for a moment I forget what I was doing.

"Finn? Are you there?" she asks again.

"Yes . . ." I hesitate between stepping out of line and hanging up the phone because, these feelings are so fucking foreign and I honestly don't know how to handle them.

"I need you."

Chapter
TWENTY-FOUR

Stevie

THE DESERT PASSES LIKE A BLUR OUTSIDE OF THE WINDOW OF FINN'S rental car. Endless dirt and trees interspersed with small towns where I could never imagine living.

But I don't really see them. All I see is the woman's face who claims to be my mother. All I hear are her words saying my father might not be my father. All I feel is hollow and confused and simply put, devastated.

"Stevester? Where are you?" my daddy shouts down the hall as I bury my face in my pillow to hide my sobs. "Stevie?"

My door opens and his sigh fills my room moments before the bed dips beside me and his massive hand spreads over the whole of my back in comfort.

"Do you want to tell me why you're upset?"

"I'm not." My breath hitches, but I think he'll believe me.

"Mrs. Martin called and said something happened at school today."

"I don't like school." I bite my bottom lip to fight back the tears that threaten to fall again.

"Yes, you do." He presses a kiss to the back of my head and that only makes me want to cry harder.

"No, I don't. Everyone is mean."

"What happened?" he asks again.

"Jill told me that I couldn't go to the Mother's Day Tea tomorrow because I didn't have a mom. That my mom hated me so much she ran away from

me." I promised myself I wasn't going to tell him. That I was going to keep this a secret so he wouldn't be sad, but it burned a hole right through my chest.

His hand stills on my back and I know I've hurt his feelings, but I don't know how to make it better.

"Stevester. Look at me." Those giant hands of his pick me up and set me in his lap so that his arms are wrapped around me squeezing me tight, letting me know whatever it is that it'll be okay. He puts his finger under my chin to guide my head up so I'm forced to look in eyes the same color as mine. "Your mom leaving had nothing to do with you. Do you hear me? Mary Johnson's missing out on knowing her incredibly special daughter, Stevie. She doesn't know just how special you are, and that is her fault. But it's not because she didn't want you. I know you want a mommy and it hurts that you don't have one, but I promise to do everything I can so you don't feel left out."

I nod but the hurt doesn't go away.

I nodded and then laughed till my tummy hurt when he walked into my class for the Mother's Day Tea the next morning with a pink, sparkly wig on, a muumuu over his usual tennis shorts and polo shirt, a wand that he used to sprinkle fairy dust (aka glitter) with, and a platter of the most atrocious-looking homemade cookies I've ever seen. But he sat on the floor crisscross applesauce with us kids showing us how to drink with our pinkies out while the other moms were too stuffy to be like him.

And he might have made sure to sprinkle Jill with fairy dust a few times for good measure.

The car stops. Finn asks me if I need anything. I respond in silence, his sigh heavy as I assume he stares at me before getting out to pump gas without me ever responding. People walk to and from the McDonalds across the street. A tumbleweed is stuck between a telephone pole and transformer box. A semi pulls its Jake Brake somewhere on the highway next to us.

Is it true?

Has my mother been trying to be a part of my life and my dad paid her off to keep her away? *Why?* Why would he do that to a little girl who was starving for a mother and the affection only a mother can give?

"*Dammit, Stevie. You can do better than that!*" My dad paces from one side of the court to the next. His racket is in one hand while he adjusts his ball cap with his other, frustration evident in his posture and the way he swings his racket as if he's talking to me and not on the other side of the net.

I sigh and roll my head back, the hangover pounding like a drumbeat in my head. I thought I was hiding it better than I obviously am.

"*You want to tell me what the hell has gotten into you this morning? Why you're late to the ball? Why your backhand is weak? Why you're huffing and puffing like a chain-smoker?*"

"*I didn't sleep well,*" I lie, hands on my hips, temper firing.

"*Didn't sleep well?*" He serves the ball hard and fast at me. I'm unprepared and give a half-assed attempt to reach it. "*Or snuck out and got drunk with Jordan and Vivi even though you're only sixteen years old?*"

He rockets another serve at me before I can even recover from the shock that he knows about last night. The ball hits my leg and I grunt in response, refusing to show any sign of weakness, because isn't that what he's getting at?

"*You don't think I didn't hear you?*" Another ball to the far corner of the court. "*You don't think I don't know where you are all the time for your own safety?*" One that has me running back the other way. "*Maybe I let you go so I could teach you a lesson.*" An ace that whooshes right past me. "*Maybe I wanted to show you how being careless affects your game.*"

I put my hands on my knees, my chest burning, my head pounding, and my gut churning.

"*Maybe I thought—*"

"*God forbid I'm a normal teenager,*" I scream at him, not caring who is on other courts nearby or what they hear. "*God forbid I have a life outside of—*"

"*You don't get to be a normal teenager when you're one of the best goddamn tennis players in the world,*" he shouts back followed by another ball that gets past me.

Tyrant.

And I'm well aware what the balls on the ground, the missed balls on the court, behind me mean—wind sprints. A sprint for each one missed. A way to drill into my head that we don't miss.

Asshole.

"Fuck you," I mutter under my breath, hating him with everything I am. The missed school dances and football games and trips to hang out at the mall. All the rites of passage that most other teenagers in America get that I don't.

It's always one more game. One more session. One more mile. One more fucking everything because it's never good enough for him.

"What was that?" he asks, his chuckle a low hum that says he knows exactly what it was. "Athletes like you don't get to be careless. Champions like you don't get days off. Once-in-a-lifetime players like you need to always be at their best."

I hate you.

Am I really his flesh and blood? Have I lived a life believing one thing and now am all but begging fate for it to be true? Because he's all I've ever known, all I've ever loved, and I need to feel that unbroken bond right now. I need to know that my smile is in fact his, and that weird birthmark on my thigh isn't just a coincidence because he has one there too. *Had. He* had *one just like me.*

That connection was my tether. My north star.

I hiccup back the sob that threatens from realizing that all I've ever thought was true, just might not be.

The sun is blazing hot and the one thing that stands out to me be-sides the absolute silence is the feel of a lone bead of sweat trickling down the length of my spine.

I don't see the people packed in the grandstands.

I don't notice the cameras or hear the click of their shutters as I walk toward the service line and take a deep, measured breath.

This is it.

This is my chance to serve and win a point.

This is when I earn my spot in history as one of the few to win a Calendar Year Grand Slam—four consecutive Grand Slams in a row.

"Game on, Stevester. Let's go."

I hear his voice from his place in the stands and the crowd around me chuckles. I hear it then I drown it out, but I'm more settled now. The words my father has uttered to me before every huge match point have become a thing the audience expects—and something I need to hear.

I don't glance his way, but I adjust my visor in my unspoken way to let him know I heard him.

The chair umpire says, "Quiet, please," in his hushed tone as I bounce the ball once, then twice.

Another deep breath as I glance up to see my opponent, Marvela, bouncing back and forth on her feet, anticipating the location of my serve.

I toss the ball up with one hand and swing my racket overhead with the other. The ball launches across the net and Marvela is caught flatfooted, thinking I was going to serve the opposite way. Ace.

The crowd explodes in a cacophony of sound that I can't so much as hear as I can feel in the rumbling in my chest.

It's over.

It's done.

I did it.

No, we did it.

And as much as I want to drop to my knees in sheer exhaustion, I need to find him. I need to find the man who pushed me when I didn't think I could go any further. Who loved me when my mother decided she didn't. And who has been my everything my entire life.

I look up through the sea of people to find my dad grinning from ear to ear. There are tears in his eyes. Tears I used to think made him a silly man when I was little but have now learned are charged with pride. In me.

He wraps his arms around me and pulls me against him. "You did it. Unbelievable. You did it."

There's an odd sense of amnesia at this point. A forgiveness of all the pain, the sweat, and the tears that got me to this point. Of the resentment over how hard he pushed me. Of the anger I had over all the things I've missed out on.

It's a temporary amnesia.

One that comes with each win, with each victory achieved, before I return to reality to feel it again and again.

"I'm so proud of you, Stevester."

The anger comes in waves as the car brakes with the afternoon flow of traffic. At the woman who might be my mom. At how she might have tricked my dad my entire life into believing he's something to me that he's not. At how I might not belong to anybody.

The tears slide slowly and solemnly down my cheeks. One after another, each one etching through the path of the one before it. Each one a reminder how quickly life can change.

My chest hurts and my head swims with thoughts that seem clear and then grow cloudy just as quickly.

The only thing I take solace in is that even though Liam Lancaster might not be my father by blood, he still *fathered* me. He was still the one who taught me how to tie my shoes, to ride a bike. The man who kissed my owies when they happened and who laid down the law, even though I still resent him for it.

He is the reason I'm here today even when he's not, and I struggle with how I can love him as much as I begrudge him.

Finn asks questions that I don't respond to. Do I need to use the bathroom? Am I hungry or thirsty? Do I need anything from him?

I just keep staring out the window as if the vastness will give me answers when I know it won't.

And I keep reminding myself that Finn came when I had no one else to call. He came to my hotel room and didn't ask a single question. He simply gathered me up in his arms like a child before using service elevators to sneak me out the back of the hotel to a car he had rented so I didn't have to deal with any other reporters.

He came back even after he quit on me.

The thought floats in and out of my memories so much so that it's easier when we get wherever we're going in San Diego to close my eyes and pretend to be asleep.

The sky is overcast and the breeze smells like the sea, but I don't want to talk or look anyone in the eyes so, it's so much easier to keep them closed.

To let Finn lift me out of the car like a sleeping child and take me inside. To feel his arms around me as if he were my protector. To not have to be tough right now when all I want to do is fall apart.

And to allow myself the grace to do just that if I want to.

Chapter
TWENTY-FIVE

Stevie

Vivi: I'm worried about you. Are you okay? Do you need me to come there?

Jordan: We will be there if you need us, okay, hon?

Me: I just need time to think.

Vivi: We're here for you. Always.

Jordan: Love you.

Chapter
TWENTY-SIX

Finn

"Again, thank you." Carson's voice is soft, grateful, his concern evident in every word he's spoken over the past two days.

I walk farther out on the deck that overlooks the Pacific Ocean and away from where Stevie sits just inside the house. Where she hasn't really moved from in the past forty-eight hours.

"I couldn't leave her there." It's all I say, and I'm still not certain what to make of those five words. My decision. Nor do I acknowledge how seeing her like a hollow shell of herself feels either.

I glance over at Stevie sitting on the couch, her face toward the ocean. Her skin is pale, her cheeks look gaunt, and her eyes now look too big for her face. Her hair is pulled up in a topknot and she has the same tracksuit she had on when I picked her up two days ago.

"We need to cancel all the events you planned for her. Give her downtime to—"

"I'll take care of it."

The line falls silent as we both struggle with what it feels like to feel helpless.

"So what now?" Carson asks, breaking the silence. "The story is taking on a life of its own without her making a statement."

"Hell if I know." I chuckle softly, knowing she can't hear me. "I figured I'd give her a couple of days to process then force her to address it in one way or another. Her phone is dead. She hasn't picked it up since we left the hotel so I know she's not seeing the chaos."

"Chaos that's only being noticed because Stevie is who she is."

"Exactly," I murmur.

"What are your thoughts on this Mary Johnson lady?"

"Don't you know? I thought you'd be able to tell me."

"I know nothing about her. I called Liam's lawyer for some insight. The same one who had informed me of Liam's wish for me to manage Stevie after he passed."

"And?"

"He's handled Liam's affairs for years. The man could have been full of bullshit when he told me he'd never heard of her—attorney-client privilege and all of that—but you know I can read people pretty well, and I genuinely think he was telling the truth."

"*Shit.*"

"That pretty much sums it up." He chuckles in frustration. "So what's your take on this woman?"

"My first thought was that Stevie needed to demand a DNA test but then I wondered what would that help? If she is her mom, will that only make the hurt worse? If she isn't, then this whole farce could be over but Stevie would still be hurt." I take a seat as a huge swell crashes on the beach below.

"And the payments? She says she has records of them."

"Payments can be made for a lot of reasons—alimony, business reasons, to keep her out of his daughter's fucking life because she's a washed-up druggie needing her next fix. That's my bet. That this is all about the money."

"Mine too. How do we make this go away?"

"Let it die? Keep her here and let the news cycle move on? If we don't give the fire oxygen, it will die. You're the one who taught me that."

"You're fine with her staying there? This coming from the man who walked away from her?"

But I went back.

"I can work from here and she can train away from the public eye. There's a private tennis court here that Kellen can work with her on, and I have a weight room downstairs she can lift in. Her bodyguards have already taken up residence in the granny flat next door. I mean, is it ideal? No. But it's going to have to work."

There is a beat of silence. "Why?"

And I know that why means a million things. Why did I walk away originally? Why did I come back? Why have I let her get to me when I won't admit it?

"Because like with you, there's just something about this woman— even at her wildest—that gets under your skin. Something you can't put your finger on but that you can't walk away from."

"I trust you." It's three words, but ones I've never heard uttered from his lips. And they simultaneously fill me with pride and terror that I'm going to mess this up.

We finish talking about a few more things and when I hang up, Stevie is still sitting there like a ghost on my couch.

I move toward her. Her eyes track me until I take a seat beside her but she doesn't say a word.

"Can I get you anything?" I ask.

No response. Nothing.

I'm not good with emotional women. Tears unnerve me. Hysteria annoys me. But there is one thing that Stevie has taught me—a lack of emotion terrifies me.

You don't know what the other person is thinking or feeling. You don't know how to react or respond and you spend every interaction second-guessing if you did the right thing.

But Stevie looks so damn sad. So confused. So I sit back next to her, wrap my arm around her shoulder, and pull her in close to my side.

She doesn't say anything at all but rather rests her head against my shoulder. I don't know how long we sit like this, with me giving comfort I'm probably not suitable to give, but at least I don't feel as helpless as I did.

At least I feel like I'm trying to do something.

Time passes in waves crashing on the beach and the buzz of my cell phone on the table across the room, but we don't move, nor do we speak. It's a peaceful sound. Odd how I've never stopped long enough to notice that in all the times I've been coming here.

The waves have just been there. A constant in the background. But now . . . now they're soothing. Peaceful. Exactly what Stevie needs as we sit here, somehow giving each other something that we can't quite pinpoint but know we need nonetheless.

"Thank you." Her voice is so quiet it's almost as if she's forgotten how to use it.

I don't need her gratitude. I need her to stop being a ghost of herself.

"How about you jump in the shower and get some clean clothes on?" I press a kiss to the top of her head. "It won't fix anything but it might make you feel a bit better."

She nods.

"I think all your clothes are dirty. Do you mind if I have my housekeeper wash them and get the Las Vegas smoke out of them?" I'd thought about it yesterday but didn't want to go through her stuff without asking, and since this is the first time we've actually interacted, I figured it was worth a shot. "She can take the clothes out of your bag if that's okay, and I can give you a T-shirt and shorts to wear in the meantime."

She nods and looks up at me. I can't help but wonder what's going on in that mind of hers. If the trouble in her eyes is any indication, there's a whole hell of a lot.

"Maybe after a shower and you get something to eat, we can talk?"

Wariness etches in the lines of her face but she nods before rising from the couch. She stops at her luggage, which has been sitting untouched outside her door since we arrived, and digs through the front pockets for what looks like shampoo and conditioner before heading toward her bedroom en suite.

I head to the bags and begin to lift them when a piece of paper falls out from underneath them. I'm only being semi-nosy when I pick it up to see what it is. It's a small, white folded card with the words *Cards O' Fun* handwritten in block letters at the top and *"Have a one-night stand"* written in cursive in its center.

I don't know why I stare at those five words on the card for so long, but I do know this is the reason I met Stevie that night. This is the reason we are where we are right now.

For some reason I put the card in my back pocket and then lug her suitcases toward the laundry suite for Faith, my housekeeper, to wash them.

It's silent as Stevie picks at her grilled cheese sandwich from where she sits across the table from me.

"I know my cooking isn't great, but you can't exactly screw up a grilled cheese," I say to try and lighten the mood.

Her smile flickers momentarily. *I've missed that smile*, even if it's only a hint of the ones I've seen prior. I study her as she plays with her food. Her wet hair is up in a clip and there's slightly more color in her cheeks now. She's wearing one of my T-shirts, her tan legs crossed like a little kid on the chair where she sits.

"Stevie." I say her name and hate that she seems pained to meet my eyes. I don't understand her silence. I don't understand it, because I'd be so full of fury I'd burn everything down.

And that's what I thought she was trying to do and why I was called in by Carson . . . so this about-face is odd to me.

"I know I need to deal with it, but what if I don't want to?" she asks like a child seeking approval.

"You can't stick your head in the sand on this. She needs to be dealt with." I take a bite of my own sandwich and follow it up with a sip of wine.

"I'm ignoring *her*. Ignoring *this*."

"Just like you've been ignoring the passing of your father by trashing your reputation and almost your career?" She winces like I just slapped her across the face. I can't take my words back, nor do I think I would if I could because someone has to wake her up. Someone has to make her realize this isn't going away and she has to face it.

"Leave my father out of this," she snarls and the fire that flashes in her eyes is so damn good to see.

Fire I can handle.

Temper I can combat with.

Anything is better than her endless silence and haunted eyes.

"You're the one who called me, Stevie. I'm the one who showed up." That fire sputters with my words, and I struggle with what to do or how to do it. "Do you have a place of your own you'd like to go instead? Somewhere that you'd be more comfortable?"

Tears well in her eyes once again as she shakes her head. "Not yet. He still feels like he's everywhere there."

"Okay."

"Plus, when I'm there, everyone knows where I am, my routine. The press, the fans, the . . . just everyone. I've lived my life in front of the cameras. Every hiccup, every victory, every mistake. Can't I just have some time not to? Can't I just have clear space to breathe for a bit?"

"Take all the time you need." I lean back in my seat and look out toward the moon in the darkened sky above before looking back to her. "There's a private tennis court down the street that I've secured for you. Kellen is on standby should you want to train . . . or it would be perfectly acceptable in this situation for you to pull out of the Open next month, citing a strained back or muscle or something of the like. Of course that means your rank would fall . . ."

Her back stiffens. It's good to see it. The sight is such a juxtaposition to the meekness I've seen over the past few days and the sadness in her eyes. "I'm not pulling out of the Open. Don't bring it up again." She scoots back from her plate that she's barely touched, her voice softening. "Thank you, Finn. For bringing me here." She stands, her head down looking at her clasped hands. "I'm sorry for bringing you into this."

And with that, she leaves the dinner table and heads to her bedroom. I watch her until the door clicks, and I'm left with just my thoughts and the crash of the waves on the beach outside echoing through the house.

I finish both of our sandwiches, clean up, and am headed to my office with the rest of the bottle of wine. When I pass her room, the unmistakable sound of crying comes through the door.

I'm in complete indecision whether I should knock and offer comfort or leave her alone. I stand there for some time, my hand poised to knock, before I continue on to my office.

HARD ⊤ LOVE | 137

But even when work should fill my thoughts—new clients, merchandising deals, contract negotiations—I'm left looking out into the darkness of the night, wondering how exactly I let Stevie Lancaster get to me.

Because I did.

And I'm not quite sure what to do about it.

Chapter
TWENTY-SEVEN

Stevie

"You've reached Liam Lancaster. Leave a message and I'll get back to you when time permits."

My body aches with the deepest type of sadness when his voice fills my ears.

Then there's the beep.

"Hi, Dad. It's me. It's been a shitshow as of late—what I've been doing myself and what my supposed mother has told the world. I'm sorry. That's all I can say. You would be disappointed in me, but after beating Greshenko the other night, I realized I miss the game. There's something about it—the routine of it, the everything about it—that makes me feel closer to you.

"But more than anything, I called because I want you to know that I don't care what Mary Johnson says or doesn't say. You're my father. You always have been and you always will be. Our bond is so strong that I dare anyone to tell me we're not related."

There's a beep ending the message but I keep talking.

"I've taken a few days for myself this week and have done a lot of thinking. About who I am and who I want to be now that you're not at my side. You've always told me it's the hardest thing in the world to look at yourself and to see and then to face the truth. I've faced it, Dad. I realized that I was so busy resenting you that I forgot I still loved you." I barely choke the words out. "I realized that you did what you did to make me a better person and a stronger tennis player. I may still think of you as a tyrant some days, but I know you were busy pushing me to be everything my mom wasn't. You were trying to make me be the best me because you knew you weren't going to be here someday. So, thank you. For your sacrifices, for the nights you went to bed with indigestion because you knew you were too hard on me, but because you knew it was how I learned." I hiccup over a massive sob. "What I'd give to hear you say, 'Game on, Stevester,' one last time. I love you."

The tears come.

One after another.

The thoughts ebbing and flowing with them.

With how much he gave for me. How much I took for granted. It's only after this Mary lady has shown up that I realized how much he dedicated his life to give me mine. How much *he* sacrificed went unnoticed, because I was too busy focusing on what I was missing out on. *I never thought of him.*

The tears slide down my cheeks and my hands grip my phone and, slowly but surely, I feel lighter.

I call his voicemail again. Just to hear the message.

Just to hear his voice one more time.

Chapter
TWENTY-EIGHT

Stevie

My dad was the one who handled the heat of the media for me. He'd interrupt the harsh questions, stop the errant interviews, and protect me from the negativity.

He handled all the tough decisions about my career. The contract negotiations, the fees to be charged for endorsements, and the day-to-day management of my training.

He thought for me when I didn't want to think so that all I had to focus on was the game of tennis. The next match. Perfecting my stroke. Learning my opponents' weaknesses and strengths.

If there is one thing I've learned in the past two months—hell, in just sitting here and being forced to listen to the noise in my own head during the past five days—it's how much, in fact, my father did do for me.

And now it seems he also tried to protect me from the woman who birthed me but never cared to mother me.

I couldn't sleep last night after my tears had dried and my resolve had replaced them. Instead, I moved to the railing of this deck and watched the moon reflect off the froth of the waves and forced myself to feel.

The pain of losing my dad.

The anger regarding my supposed mom.

The fury over her coming forward and starting bullshit that after sitting back and thinking about it, changes absolutely nothing other than if she is my mom, she's made her desires more than clear—money. *At no point has she attempted to reach out to care for me. To love me in my loss. She's* just asked for money.

I forced myself to feel all the emotions when for the past two months I've numbed them with alcohol and by surrounding myself with people who wouldn't leave me alone too long so that I could.

I took the mental steps to take my life back.

And I will.

With a soft smile, I sit in one of the lounge chairs with my eyes closed and hope I didn't just make a huge mistake. It's taken me a few days and a lot of tears, but it's definitely time I face everything head-on. It's only then that I can move forward without it hanging over my head. At least I hope so, because I can't undo the steps I took moments ago. The phone call I made is over and done with.

Maybe that's why I did it. There's definitely no turning back now.

I hear Finn before I see him when he steps out on the deck. In fact, I've been listening to him in some way or another all morning as he's moved from one phone call to the next with Zoom meetings in between. There was a call to calm a client down, another to help clean up a mess someone made, and a third to introduce and possibly recruit another athlete to his firm.

There was something comforting about listening to him. The professionalism and authority with which he spoke. Two things that I'm more than certain he treated me with but that I was too wrapped up in breaking all the rules—in numbing myself—that I dismissed it *and him.*

And that was only a week ago.

It feels like a lifetime.

For some reason, I close my eyes when he approaches me from behind. Maybe I need a second more with my decision—more time for it to get set into motion—before I tell him and it can be stopped. Because that's one thing I have to give him, he hasn't pushed other than the grilled cheese night. Although I'm occupying his house and interrupting his life, he's given me the space and distance I need to figure this all out in my head.

I jolt at the sound of the splash and then startle seconds later as drops of water hit me. But when I open my eyes, Finn isn't standing there in his pool smiling at me like I expected. Instead, he's headed toward the other end of the pool. His hands slice through the water in powerful strokes, his broad back and shoulders rippling like the water and his legs kicking before his body folds in some sort of elaborate turn when he hits the end.

And when he hits the near wall, he does the same flip turn without stopping to look up.

He swims laps with a purpose that I can relate to. There's efficiency to his movements that makes me think he's not only getting his exercise in but is also solving a million problems in his head.

I may be guilty of doing something similar when I'm conditioning. Going over conversations I need to have, rehearsing them with each step, or reliving a match in my head so I can learn where I messed up.

I'm not sure how long he swims for, but I'm mesmerized by him as he does. Perhaps it's because it gives me something to concentrate on other than my own thoughts, and perhaps because my body is reacting to the sight of him when it feels like it had died over the past few days.

Or maybe it's just because sitting on a deck that overlooks the beach while watching an attractive man exercise feels like something a normal twenty-four-year-old woman would do.

And God, how I need life to feel normal.

I emit a chuckle he can't hear and lean my head back, eyes closed, so the sun that just broke through the morning clouds can warm my cheeks.

The splashing stops at some point and for reasons I don't understand, I opt yet again to keep my eyes closed. Is it because I'm embarrassed—he's seen me at my lowest these past few days—or is it simply because the man clearly stirs something in me? Something that I almost feel guilty for feeling when so many other parts of my life need to be settled.

"Can I get you anything?" Finn asks just like he has every time our paths have crossed in this house.

"No, thank you." I hold a hand up to cover my eyes and turn my head to look at him.

Huge mistake, especially as I'm trying to concentrate on my own issues and not have them clouded by a soaking-wet Finn Sanderson. One who I might add has rivulets of water sliding down his tanned, chiseled torso, and who has been more than attentive and patient with me when I definitely haven't deserved his compassion.

His eyes meet mine after he rubs his towel over his hair. "You sure?"

"Yes. I'm . . . sure." I put my face up to the sun again and close my eyes—not because I want to be left alone but because the last thing I need to do is keep staring at him. The last thing I need to do is encourage my thoughts when it comes to just how he could sate that ache his presence has created.

I'm sure he'll definitely think I've gone totally over the deep end if I go from five days of not speaking more than a few words at a time to telling him the idea of a quick, distracting fuck is what he can *do* for me.

"My mom left when I was four years old." His unexpected confession cuts through the silence and feels like a knife to my gut. My thoughts shift immediately as I hear a pain in his voice I know all too well. "I have a blurry idea of who she was and what she was like, but I often wonder if they were from the pictures I stared at so long that I willed them into my memory."

"Finn." I turn to look at him but he's staring straight ahead, finding solace in the sea like I have over the past few days.

He shrugs and it's the kind of shrug that says it doesn't bug him, but I know differently. "My dad said that one day she was there, laughing and happy and present, and then the next day he got a call from the babysitter asking him when she was going to pick me up." His tone may sound stoic, but so has mine all these years. I know the turmoil I've felt within. "He had no clue she was unhappy."

"I'm so sorry."

"I don't want you to be sorry. I just want you to know why I came back for you when you called me." He turns and looks at me for the first time and the emotion that owns his eyes is equal parts heartbreaking and strength/determination. "I want you to know that every question you've asked yourself over the past few days, I've asked myself too. I want you to know that I understand how it feels to believe your own mother doesn't love you enough to stick around and how much that can fuck with your head." He rises from his seat, puts a hand on my shoulder, and squeezes. "I just wanted you to know."

He starts to walk away, and I stare after him dumbfounded with tears in my eyes because someone understands. We may not have walked the same path to get here, but someone understands what is impossible to put into words.

"Finn." My voice is a broken croak when I say his name, but he stops and turns back around.

"Hmm?"

"Thank you for telling me. For understanding." I find words hard to come by all of a sudden, and I'm not sure why. "Earlier . . . earlier I contacted Kyle Katswa," I say, and his eyebrows raise at the name of one of the most prominent anchors at ESPN. "I'm doing an interview with him tomorrow to put this all to rest."

"You are?" He takes a step back toward me, his voice surprised.

"I am." I nod. "I'm well aware that speaking will add fuel to her fire, but I also hope it smothers it too. You are right. It's time I stop sticking my head in the sand and face this—her accusations, his death, everything—head-on." I know it won't fix the broken heart my dad's passing left me with, but it's one foot in front of the other and that's more than I've been doing.

"It's the only way you're going to be able to move forward."

"I know."

"I'm proud of you," he says.

"Let's not get ahead of ourselves yet." I chuckle. "No doubt I'll still screw something up."

He gives me a slight smile and a nod before hooking the wet towel over his neck and heading back into the house again.

Chapter
TWENTY-NINE

Stevie

CLEAN CLOTHES.

When I enter my room, my laundry is on my bed in stacks just tall enough so that the clothes don't fall over and ruin their perfectly folded corners. The fresh scent of the detergent fills the space and makes me feel more settled than I've felt all afternoon.

If it's possible to be in love with Finn's housekeeper any more than I already am, then I'm there.

It's the impending interview that has me unsettled. Sure, I've rehearsed what I want to say a million times, the main points I want to express, but what if I say something that opens me up to a slander lawsuit by Mary? What if I—

Wine.

I need wine.

Sure, it's nearing midnight but one glass might help to calm me down and settle my nerves. And if Finn happens to still be awake to run through things with, then I'll do that as well.

The lights are dim and I'm just about to the kitchen when I hear Finn's voice near the front of the house. It's a low rumble in hushed tones that I head toward, figuring he's on the phone and is just being quiet so as not to wake me up, as he has several times since I've been here.

"You don't have to be qui—" I realize my mistake a moment too late when I see Finn at the front door, his back to me, and hear a feminine laugh. "*Oh.* I didn't mean to . . ."

"It's okay." Finn retreats a step, turning so I'm met with a gorgeous brunette in a dazzling blue, sparkled dress. Her hair is a tumble of long curls and her features—eyes, nose, lips, boobs—are stunning. In that fleeting moment, insecurity rears its ugly head while I feel like she's everything that I'm not even though, from this distance, I can't even make the comparison. Yet the comparison is still there, front and center in my mind. "Kristen was just stopping by to . . ."

I force a smile on my lips praying he doesn't finish that sentence. "Of course. I'm sorry to interrupt. I was just grabbing a glass of wine and thought you might like to—never mind." The thumb I hook over my shoulder dies midmotion so that I look like an idiot trying to hitchhike. "Nice to meet you, Kristen."

"My apologies," Finn says turning back to her. "I forgot to introd—"

"Nice to meet you too . . ." Kristen says, her eyes narrowing in on me, and I don't exactly think it's because she's happy to see me there. "I'm sorry, I didn't catch your name?"

"It's—"

"Nothing," Finn stutters before staring at me and willing me to go away. "Good night." The curtness of the two words takes me by surprise and even worse is the catty smirk Kristen gives me from behind Finn.

With a purse of my lips and a nod, me and my bruised ego head back to the kitchen to drink alone.

My feelings are hurt.

I know it sounds ridiculous but they are.

If I wasn't so stressed about the interview tomorrow, I'd take a step back and realize that maybe Finn wasn't pushing me out of the way to make room for Kristen. Maybe he was pushing me away so that she didn't realize who I was and let the cat out of her no-doubt gossip-y mouth about who I was and where I was staying.

A rational me would have realized that.

But this is the jealous me who knows that there is no other reason for Kristen to show up close to midnight in her party dress, which is probably sans undergarments, other than to make an in-person booty call.

More to the point that this might not have been the first time she's done it either.

And I don't know why it bugs me so much.

Because you like him.

Of course, I like him. I wouldn't be here if I didn't, but having sex with him and scratching an itch is completely different than getting jealous when I think someone else wants to do the same thing with him.

Completely different.

"Sorry about that," Finn says as he moves into the kitchen, as if I'm not sitting over here staring at an opened wine bottle and an empty glass stewing over a woman I shouldn't give two shits about.

"I'm the one who should apologize. I didn't mean to interrupt you two. Obviously you had plans, and I didn't think twice about how me being here affected those plans and—"

"There were no plans, Stevie."

"Her heels and party dress on your doorstep at midnight say otherwise." I snort.

He chuckles. "She was quite obvious, wasn't she?"

"Just a little." I finally pour my glass and take a long sip, not caring about the sarcasm in my voice.

"Are you jealous?" he asks rounding the counter so he can see my face. I stare out the window instead, refusing to give him the satisfaction. "You *are* jealous."

"I am not. Why would I be jealous if she clearly came over for a booty call?" I roll my eyes. "We had sex. We were . . . nothing. So . . ."

"So if I were nothing with her too, then it would be okay with you?"

"I didn't say that." I snap the words out and then realize I can't take them back. He clears his throat, clearly enjoying this invisible catfight over him. I make a show of draining my glass of wine to distract him. "I'm going to bed now so just in case you have her hidden outside the door, you can sneak her into your room now."

"I'm not sneaking her anywhere, Stevie. I haven't seen her in over six months. She saw me when I went out for a jog the other day so she decided to stop by."

I turn to look at him and shrug. "Not my business. Good night, Finn."

"Good night, Jealousy."

"Good night, Jerk," I mutter to myself with a healthy slam of my bedroom door.

I don't like him.

I don't.

He can be sexy and good in bed and sweet when he needs to be all he wants, but that doesn't mean I have to like him.

Not one bit.

So then why am I lying in bed, staring at the ceiling, thinking of ways I can make him chuckle like that with me?

Chapter
THIRTY

Finn

SHE LOOKS NOTHING LIKE THE WOMAN WHO STOOD IN MY KITCHEN last night jealous over—yes, she was right—a booty call standing at my door.

The irony was that while nosy (and desperate) Kristen stood on my stoop all but throwing herself at me, it was Stevie I was thinking of. The woman who unexpectedly walked out in her pajama shorts and tank top sans makeup, who looked a hundred times sexier than Kristen in her party dress and heels.

The same woman who now is sitting behind a laptop and a ring light with a crisp, white blouse, smiling as Kyle Katswa gives an introduction to their interview. Her smile might be big, but what the camera can't see and I can, is how she's twisting her fingers in her lap.

I walk away from the room and head to my office where I have the television on so I can watch it objectively like a normal viewer would.

"So let's get right to it, Stevie," Kyle says with a warm smile. "Welcome to the show. How are you doing today?"

"I'm fine, thank you. Thanks for having me."

He sighs with a genuine compassion. "I'm not exactly sure where you want to start, so let's begin with your father. He was a driving force in your life and your career, how are you doing since his passing?"

Jesus. Talk about hitting with the emotional question right off the bat. But at the same time, it's a brilliant opener because it's something she's comfortable talking about. Something that will endear her to fans.

And as if on cue, Stevie draws in a slow, measured breath before responding. "It's been hard. Some days I wake up and reach for the phone to call him, others I don't want to get out of bed. And to be honest, to cope, I've leaned on a few vices more than I should have over the past two months, and I'm not proud of that. Sometimes, all I've wanted to do is forget even though in hindsight, I know it's not the right way to deal with grief. If that even makes sense."

Her words take me by surprise. The raw honesty in them is unexpected and yet, I know this is the woman Carson had so much faith in. This one right here laying her mistakes and possibly truths bare for all to see.

"I think most of us who have gone through the death of someone they're close to can relate."

"They can, but social media these days makes it easy for all your mistakes to be put on display for all to see. Especially when you're someone in my position and so, for all the parents out there who were upset with my missteps because their daughters look up to me, I want to apologize."

Kyle looks completely taken aback by her comments as am I. Where is the balls-to-the-wall, fuck-everybody Stevie who I first met? Was she given a media etiquette class that I wasn't aware of in the days since she's been here?

"Forgive me for being harsh when you're being so blatantly honest, Stevie, but how do the viewers, the fans, myself, know that your remarks aren't part of a publicity tour to repair your image? To try and regain back fans you've lost?"

"You don't." She shrugs. "All I can do is be honest and hope that you believe me."

"Why now? What suddenly made you want to talk to the media when you've blown them off for weeks?"

The blessing and the curse of the press. They're there when you don't want them to be, but when you need them, they'll come right back.

She's handling this brilliantly and even I'm amazed at how sincere she sounds.

"As you know, recently there have been some allegations made to other media outlets that I've yet to comment on. Added to the loss of my father"—she clears her throat and looks down at her hands before looking back at the camera— "to say they devastated me is an understatement."

"Understandably." He nods. "And that's why you agreed to this interview."

Stevie nods. "For me, my first reaction was to want to run and hide— which I'm not very proud of—but that's what I did. But the hiding not only allowed me, but also *forced* me to really think and put things in perspective . . . such as my recent behavior."

My phone is buzzing like crazy in my pocket, but I toss it on the sofa in my office, completely entranced by the woman on the TV in front of me.

"And that's why we're here."

"Yes. In the past, my father was the one who handled all of this kind of stuff. With him gone, facing these things forced me to grow up."

"When you say your father—"

"He was my father," Stevie asserts. "I don't care what this lady—"

"Mary Johnson."

"—says. Liam Lancaster was my father every second of every minute of every day. For her to insinuate that he isn't or wasn't, is probably one of the cruelest things someone could ever accuse or attest. To try and take that from me after his death is not something a mother would do to her child."

"Since you brought it up, let's go there. Do you believe Mary Johnson is your mother?"

"I don't care if she is or isn't. She *might* even be the person named on my birth certificate. While my father, Liam, was there every second, she wasn't. Even if I did a DNA test to prove her allegations to be true, that she is in fact the woman who birthed me, she would still mean nothing to me. A true mother would move heaven and earth to see their child if they wanted to. She didn't."

"That brings up another point. Mary states that she couldn't contact you because that was part of the conditions of her settlement with your dad."

"You mean the monthly payments she alleges he made to her? Cash payments that haven't been proven? Isn't that proof enough why she's talking publicly at this point? If she wanted a relationship with her supposed daughter, then all she had to do was reach out to my people. My father is dead so whatever agreement they had between them would be null and void."

"You said 'isn't that proof why she's talking publicly.' Can you clarify what you mean by that?"

"She wants money. Plain and simple."

"If she hasn't contacted you like you say, then how can you be so sure?"

Stevie emits a disbelieving laugh before taking a moment to collect her words. "Just like your audience has to make a judgment call on if my apology during this interview is sincere or not without even meeting me, I had to do the same with this woman."

"And you conclude she's after a payoff."

"Hasn't she already gotten one? From the television network who released her exclusive interview? From the tabloids who have her tell-all story? She's been paid. Regardless, if my father sent her checks or not, she won't get a dime from me."

"But let's stop right there. If he was in fact paying her a repeated sum, then doesn't that reinforce the fact that she is in fact your mother?"

"My dad was my fiercest protector. If he thought someone was going to hurt me or my career in any way, then he would have done everything he could to keep me safe."

"But that means he might have also kept you from having a mother."

She swallows forcibly and I know that question got to her. Just as it would have gotten to me. But she takes her time choosing her words before answering. "Clearly, he was right in his decision, seeing as her first steps toward me after twenty-plus years were through the media to try and destroy everything I've ever known to be true. It's almost as if she thought using the press against me was a form of blackmail—that I'd be afraid she'd ruin my image—and that would scare me enough to pay to shut her up."

"That's a big accusation."

"*Just as hers are*," Stevie says with a steely resolve that leaves me shaking my head.

"So I guess a live-for-television family reunion is out of the question?" Kyle asks with a laugh.

Stevie joins in but then her expression becomes serious. "Like I said, I have zero desire to ever meet Mary Johnson and if I had in the past, she killed every possibility of it by the things she said."

Kyle nods and lets the weight of Stevie's statement settle. "So what now for Stevie Lancaster?"

"I move on, but I don't forget." She gives a bittersweet smile that tugs on my heart. "Now with my head on straight, I start training for the Open with a vengeance and then maybe, every once in a while, do something spontaneous that makes me feel alive."

"I like the sound of that." Kyle leans back in his chair. "On a closing note, tell me something about your father. Something you learned from him or that you want people to know about him."

"He was my best friend," she murmurs.

"That's sweet, but there is no way that even through the teenage years that you two were that close. I have a fifteen-year-old daughter and I think she likes me about one minute out of every sixty."

Stevie laughs and then her smile falls slowly. "The truth, Kyle? The truth is when I was a teenager, I hated him some days almost as much as I loved him. I didn't understand why I had to miss my senior prom or why I couldn't participate in senior ditch day. I hated him because he didn't think any boy was good enough and therefore when the few girlfriends I had were out living it up, kissing boys and figuring their dating lives out, I thought of him as more of a tyrant than my father and coach. Maybe that's why I went a little crazy after he died. Maybe that was my attempt to live on the wild side I never had the chance to live." She smiles softly as tears well in her eyes. "The funny thing is, trying to do that only served to prove him right. Now I'm behind training for the Open."

"So you are playing the Open?"

"I haven't missed one yet."

"You'll get there. I'm sure of it," Kyle says as Stevie nods shyly. "I want to thank you for sitting down with me. I know that couldn't have been easy for you."

"It was important for me to say my piece so that I can move forward, so thank you for letting me do that."

"Best of luck to you."

Then the feed switches off and Kyle moves on to his next story behind his anchor desk. I turn the TV off but stay seated where I am and wonder where the hell all of that just came from. I mean, if allowing Stevie Lancaster to sit alone for five days with her thoughts produces an earnest, believable, honest interview such as the one she just gave, then I think she needs to be left to her thoughts more often.

I don't know how long I sit there ignoring the buzzing of my phone on the couch beside me, but when I look up, Stevie is standing in the doorway studying me.

She cocks her head to the side and is silent for a beat. "Well?"

I give a disbelieving shake of my head. "Are you okay?" It's not what I meant to say. I meant to tell her she was brilliant and I was proud of her for everything she said, but I also know saying what she said probably took a toll on her.

She inhales a shaky breath. "I wouldn't have said it if I weren't."

"And so just like that, things are crystal clear and okay?"

"To the public, yes. To me, I'm still a major work in progress, but at least I know the answers. And I know where I need to get to."

"No more stripper poles or strip poker or trying to lose me?" I ask, a ghost of a smile on my lips as she takes a seat beside me and leans her head on my shoulder.

"Does that mean you no longer quit on me?"

"It means that you're welcome to stay here and train for the Open." That's not what she asked because frankly, I don't have an answer. I had a reason for walking away. A damn good one.

Or at least I thought so at the time.

And then I invited her to live with me for two months.

My logic isn't exactly sane at this point.

"Thank you," she says softly. "For coming back to get me. For letting me stay here. For telling me about your mom. Somehow, that made it easier to say what I had to say."

"Today was all you," I say, resting my cheek on the side of her head in a rare show of empathy. "And you did one hell of a job, Stevie. Incredible actually. I'm proud of you."

Chapter
THIRTY-ONE

Finn

"AND YOU WONDER WHY I BROUGHT YOU ON BOARD TO HANDLE HER?" Carson chuckles into the phone. There is the sound of a steel drum somewhere in the background and laughter. The fucker probably has his feet up on a wicker footstool and someone serving him cocktails if my hunch is correct.

"Took you long enough to call. Let me guess, you're in some tropical paradise where the cell service sucks and the Wi-Fi is intermittent?"

His chuckle is all I need as confirmation. "You're a goddamn genius, son. That interview was perfection. Absolute perfection. How'd you pull that off?"

"I didn't. She did."

"I'm sure you did something to prompt it."

"I'd love to take the credit." And normally I would, but for some reason, I can't on this one. "I didn't do anything other than give her time to think."

"But you got her the interview that was heard around the world."

"She did that. She made the call and set it up without me even knowing."

"Take the credit, Sanderson. Didn't I teach you anything?" He laughs.

"Have another Mai Tai."

"Don't mind if I do." He emits a belly laugh. "Is this the part where you tell me your job is done and now, she's all mine?"

"This is the part where . . ." I don't have an answer for him because his question just threw me completely. *Is that what I want?* To be rid of Stevie after all is said and done? I clear my throat, acutely aware that Carson is listening carefully to my silence and drawing his own conclusions. "This is the part where I told her she could stay here and train until the Open."

"And then you're done with her," Carson finishes for me.

"Yes. Sure. I've got a full plate with clients."

"Uh-huh." And there it is, the sound every son knows from his father, and Carson is no exception when it comes to me.

"*Uh-huh, nothing,* old man." I shake my head. "There's nothing to see here."

"Never said there was." He chuckles again. "You made me proud, son."

I hang up with him a few minutes later feeling accomplished and strangely content from Carson's praise.

Those are words I don't ever think I heard my dad utter. I knew he was proud of me, that's why he showed up to my games and told everyone he knew about me, but he never showed it. Instead, he gave sharp criticism that only seemed to get worse when I had my shoulder surgery and had to give up the game I loved.

Those criticisms increased substantially when he saw me thriving under the tutelage of Carson. It's amazing what praise can do in place of constant criticism.

I think all that negativity is what put him in an early grave. That and maybe a lot of guilt over the bullshit he ingrained in me when it came to women.

"Bullshit?" I mutter as I lean against my kitchen counter and look out toward the darkening sky.

Since when did I start thinking of it as bullshit?

Are all these years of Carson telling me my theories on women are full of shit finally breaking through to me?

C'mon, Finn. You know your old man was full of shit, right? Not all women leave. Not all women are assholes.

Seriously? You're just going to up and dump her just like that? She made you happy.

It's not a crime to be in a relationship, Sanderson. Hell isn't going to freeze over, you know.

One of these days, son, you're going to learn that life is so much more fun when you have someone by your side.

The comments echo over and over in my head.

Christ.

Carson may not be setting Stevie and me up in the traditional sense, but it sure as hell feels like he's been working on this for a long-ass time.

"Honey, I'm home," Stevie calls out seconds before the slam of the front door. Her footsteps grow near before I hear, "And how was your day, dear?"

Stevie walks into the house in a plain white tennis skirt and a pink sports bra. It's something I've seen her in plenty of times and yet, for some reason today, it stops me in my tracks. The woman is gorgeous. Dressed up, dressed down, completely sweaty from hours of working out and training—she is just a natural beauty.

"What?" she asks, her eyes narrowing as she stares at me.

"Nothing. Sorry." I pause. Regroup. "How was training?"

"Good. Great." She moves into the kitchen and grabs an apple from the counter and takes a bite of it. "Kellen is bitching to me about some habit I picked up on my backhand but I think we worked through it." She shrugs. "Or we will by the time I need it to be right."

"Sounds promising."

"I'll get it right. What about you?" she asks talking around a mouthful of apple. "How was your day? Did you negotiate any earth-shattering contracts or win over any new clients?"

I blow out a sigh and lean against the counter thinking about my call from Chase Kincade today. "Possibly." I take a sip of my beer. "I'm trying to steal a pitcher away from another agent and it's proving to be more difficult than I had anticipated."

"Is this the part where you find some dirt on the other agent and use it as blackmail to get the new client?"

"Jesus," I bark out in a laugh.

"Isn't that what you guys do? Play dirty?" Her smile is mischievous and her eyes look more alive than the first time I met her.

It's good to see.

"Well, this particular agent I have a lot of info on, but I won't be using it against her."

"Her?"

It's as if that singular pronoun is a calling card to Stevie.

"Yes. *Her.*"

Stevie eyes me, her smile growing wider, as she moves around the counter toward me. "Finn? Did you sleep with this *her*?"

"I never kiss and tell," I deadpan and then laugh when she pushes playfully against my chest.

"You did, didn't you? And now you're trying to steal her client?"

"As a matter of fact, yes. To both questions." I shrug nonchalantly. "It's just . . . it's complicated."

"So let me see, you had a thing with this hot female agent—"

"How do you know she's hot?"

"Because it's you," she says with a chuckle. "And—"

"And while I may have dirt on her, the dirt she has on me is way worse," I confess, my own smile playful.

Stevie narrows her eyes as she studies me. "You cheated on her, didn't you?"

The look on my face must give away the answer. "*Finn!* You're a bastard." This time when she swats at me, I grab her wrist and somehow, we end up chest to chest, our faces inches apart.

The rise of her chest in the fall of mine.

Her smile is still on her lips but her eyes darken as we stare at each other. "I was," I murmur. "I had my reasons for what I did. Good, bad, or wrong, I did what I did, and I've made amends with her over it."

"And she's okay with it?" she asks in disbelief, as her eyes dart down to my lips and then back up to my eyes.

"She's happily married so I think she moved on just fine."

"*Oh.* You're still a bastard, though," she all but whispers as my pulse roars in my ears.

"I know."

"I found some fresh cherries at the market," Faith says.

Stevie and I jump apart like two kids getting caught kissing, seconds before she walks in with bags of groceries.

"I know I said I was gone for the day, but that farmers' market was set up down the street and I just couldn't resist," she continues on, oblivious to the kiss she almost interrupted. "I know how much you like cherries, Finn."

Stevie lifts her eyebrows at the comment and swallows her laugh with a cough. "Thank you, Faith. I'm going to go take a shower." Her eyes meet mine and a smile toys at the corners of her lips. "Enjoy your cherries, Finn."

I watch her ass sway as she walks away. Faith prattles on as she often does. I half listen and respond when required as she puts the groceries away, but my mind is definitely on the woman taking a shower.

The one I'd like to be lathering up with my own hands.

And then it hits me.

I have a woman living under my roof who makes me think dirty thoughts as much as I enjoy talking to her.

Well, almost as much.

A woman who asked about my day when she didn't have to.

A woman who I felt compelled to give a valid reason as to why I cheated on a good woman like Chase Kincade.

A woman I enjoy sparring with, sharing life with, who challenges me on every level.

One of these days, son, you're going to learn that life is so much more fun when you have someone by your side.

Maybe Carson is right—all women aren't like my mother.

Maybe it's time to call the noise my dad put in my head *bullshit.*

To acknowledge that women *shouldn't* be used and discarded.

Because Stevie Lancaster is a woman who *should never be used nor discarded.*

And that realization scares the fuck out of me.

Chapter THIRTY-TWO

Stevie

THE BIKINI I CHOSE TO WEAR WASN'T WITHOUT THOUGHT.

It's bright yellow and hugs me perfectly in all the right places while showcasing all of the other ones I want to be showcased.

Especially after that long cold shower where I imagined the hands soaping up my breasts and between my legs were Finn's and not mine.

Jesus, the man can get me riled up in every sort of way.

He walked away from my kiss once.

He left after we had sex.

Yes, that was mutual and probably for the best, so why can't I get the man out of my mind?

I'm curious though, where is he going to go now that we're all but living together in his house?

I saw him look at me. I know he wants me just as badly as I want him . . . so what's holding him back?

"I learned a long time ago not to get personal with clients."

But has that changed?

I don't want to resort to the same tactics as before, because I pursued him out of spite—*anger*—but does he want me? Are things different now? *Am I different now?*

I mess with my hair a bit more, trying to see if up or down is better, and I realize I'm feeling a bit more like myself than I have in the longest of times. Confident in myself.

The interview went great—I said what I needed to say—and I've since removed all social media from my phone so I could shut out the chatter. I don't care what Mary Johnson has said in response. My father's lawyer has confirmed that there was nothing in his will that earmarked funds for the woman or even acknowledged her existence.

And considering my father made sure to have my management situation spelled out with Carson, I'm sure if Mary were a concern, he would have done the same.

So to me, that situation is done and over with.

Add to that, my training has gone well. I'm not as rusty as I expected to be and even though Kellen keeps telling me I am, he's nowhere near as good as my father was at hiding his satisfaction of where I'm at.

It feels good to be back in the groove again.

It'd feel better if Finn had acted on that desire I saw swimming in his eyes in the kitchen.

"Maybe it's time I give him a little push," I murmur as I check myself in the mirror before heading out to the patio where I can hear Finn on the phone right now. "Because not only is Finn Sanderson sexy and desirable . . . *he's good.*"

Chapter
THIRTY-THREE

Finn

"THAT'S NOT HOW THIS WORKS, DEANDRE. I KNOW IT SEEMS ILLOGICAL, but I can't just go and . . ." And all thoughts fade from my head as Stevie walks out onto the deck and heads toward the railing overlooking the ocean.

The bikini. Her body. The memory of what she tastes like. Feels like.

"Finn? You okay?" my client says in my ear.

"Yes." No, I'm not. "I, uh . . ."

"Clearly you're otherwise occupied." His chuckle fills my ear. "That's what I get for calling after hours."

"No, I'm fine." I blink as if it's going to rid the image of Stevie bending over to pick something up off the deck out of my head.

It didn't.

"So, the answer to your question," I say, trying to concentrate on my running back and not on her, "is that we have to wait. I know it's not what you want to hear, but it's how the game is played."

"Shit."

"I know. Sit tight though. We should have an answer in the next few days. Or at least that's what I was promised."

"All right. I appreciate you answering even though it's so late."

"Not a problem."

I end the call and look down at my phone in my hand for a beat before tossing it on the table beside me. Looking back up, I take a moment to appreciate the sight of Stevie.

Her body is honed like an athlete's but somehow hasn't lost the curves of a woman. And that bikini—*man, that bikini*—is sexy and seductive and the current reason my dick is hardening in my board shorts.

"Sorry. Did I interrupt you?" she asks as she looks over her shoulder. The coy smile on her lips and her eyes roaming down to my thighs and then back up a clear indication that the woman came out here to finish what we started earlier.

And Christ how I want to finish it.

But how do I do that when I'm living with her? When I can't walk away when we're done because I'll have to see her in the kitchen over a glass of water at midnight or wake up the next morning and see her over breakfast?

That's not who I am.

That's not me.

I've never done that before nor do I intend to.

"No. It's fine." I smile as she takes a step toward me. "You're fine."

"Okay. I know it's a lot to have someone in your space all the time so I'm just trying to make sure I stay out of yours as much as possible."

"I told you to make yourself at home," I say as I take a step toward the railing. "You're not in my way."

But you sure as hell suck up the oxygen in every room you walk into.

"Please let me know if I am."

My patio is huge, but all of a sudden it feels like it's shrinking with Stevie and me on a collision course somewhere in the middle.

I'm more than certain I can handle the impact.

I'm not so certain I'd be able to handle the aftermath.

"How were your cherries?" she asks, that smirk turning lopsided as she turns to face me, her elbows tucked behind her on the railing, the whole of her body on full display. "Should I be jealous that Faith knows your favorite things and I don't?"

I twist my lips and shake my head. "I have a lot of favorite things."

"Like?"

"Like good cherries, a great underdog story, carrot cake with home-made cream cheese frosting . . ." I purse my lips as I think of what else I like. "A good glass of whiskey, negotiating a great contract for a deserving client, and warm summer nights on this patio right here."

"I didn't expect a few of those."

"Like?" I step up to the railing beside her but keep a few feet between us for my own sanity's sake. The last thing I need is to smell that subtle scent she wears or to have her arm brush against mine when I've yet to decide what I want to do here.

My cock definitely knows what it wants, but I'm trying to be smart here. I'm trying to figure out my own confused head—*the one above my shoulders*—before I complicate things more.

"Like carrot cake."

I chuckle. "Never underestimate what a lot of sugar can do to something."

"I'll keep that in mind." She takes a step toward me, and I swear my breath hitches like a teenage schoolboy anticipating his first kiss. It's ridiculous. It's awesome. "Finn?"

"Hmm?" I ask as my eyes dart down to her mouth before I lean forward and frame her face in my hands. "This is going to be a bad idea."

"Sometimes those are the best kinds of ideas," she murmurs just as my lips meet hers.

It starts out as a soft sigh of a kiss, almost as if it's going to take us a minute to reacquaint our lips and tongues—*even though the last time I kissed her has replayed through my head way too much.*

But it's way better than memory serves. Her taste. Her touch. The soft sound she makes in the back of her throat.

Christ Almighty, this woman is a drug.

I think one more kiss will be enough but then my hands are on her and it becomes one more touch. One more taste. One more fucking everything until I'm drowning in her.

But I don't care because it feels like we've been doing a slow dance of seduction for weeks and goddamn, I'm ready to get pulled under.

"Finn," she moans against my lips when my fingers hook her suit to the side and find her slick with desire. "Just fucking take me already, will you?"

I don't need any other words to spur me on.

My laugh is muffled by her kiss.

"You walk around this house in your dress shirts or board shorts—both do things to me I'm not proud of, Sanderson—so you better be the one to start doing *me*."

"What things?" I tuck my fingers into her as she gasps and digs her nails into my shoulders. "Dirty things? Please tell me it's dirty things."

Her laugh is part moan, part chuckle as my mouth closes over hers again. "So, so dirty." She lowers herself to her knees, and I groan in anticipation as her hands free my cock from my shorts. She kisses the tip of my head, and it jerks in reflex. "You're in that fancy office of yours on a call with a client when I walk in. *Naked*." Her lips close around me and the warm, wet heat of her mouth is like fucking heaven, hell, and everything in between.

"That's a good start."

"You fist a hand in the back of my hair and bend me over the desk so that I'm spread wide for you to see. And then you fuck me from behind." She lowers her lips over the length of my shaft, each inch disappearing into her mouth until I feel it hit the back of her throat. She lets it sit there for a moment, allowing me to enjoy the sensation until she comes back off it with a loud popping sound when the suction breaks.

"That can be arranged," I pant. Her words are seductive, but I'm finding it hard to concentrate on them while absorbing every fucking ounce of pleasure her mouth is offering.

"And while you're doing that and talking to your client, almost growling low in your throat, I'm busy rubbing my clit just like I'm doing now."

I glance down and meet her eyes just in time to see her slide two fingers in her mouth before moving them beneath the yellow triangle of her bikini bottoms. Her eyes flutter shut as her hand begins to move. But it's the moan she emits when she sucks me into her mouth again, the one that vibrates from the crest of my cock all the way down to my balls, that has every single one of my nerve endings singing with pleasure.

She slides her lips and her free hand up and down the length of me, each twist of her hand sending shockwaves through me.

"And when I'm close, as I'm bent over your desk"—her breath is labored as her own fingers work her up—"you'll have to clamp a hand over my mouth because I'll come so hard that your client will hear."

She licks her tongue around the ridge of my cock before sucking on just the tip. My body revolts, begging me to come now and not wait for the velvet of her pussy.

I hit the back of her throat again, and I fight the urge to hold the back of her head still so I can fuck her mouth until I'm good and empty.

"God, you taste so incredible." Then she sucks me back into her mouth and moans around my cock.

And that's it. That's my undoing. Her praise. Her tongue. Her fingering herself.

I fist a hand in her hair and pull her head back so she's forced to look up at me. "You better stop or I'm going to fuck you hard and fast," I growl.

A coy smile plays on her parted lips. "I'm counting on it." And this time, when she pulls me between her two lips, she keeps her eyes locked on mine as her cheeks hollow out and she sucks.

My hand tightens and it takes everything I have to jerk my cock from her mouth and not finish.

"*You*," I say. A smile turns up the corners of her lips as my cock waits just inches from her mouth.

"What are you going to do about it?"

I'm hauling her up to her feet within seconds and crashing my mouth against hers. I can't think of anything but the end game. I can't focus on anything else but her.

We crash into the chaise lounge.

"This is just sex." She laughs.

We bump against the doorway into the house.

"Just sex," I agree against her lips.

We knock something off a table.

"Then give me the fucking sex."

We don't stop until we're rolling around on the floor of the great room like we're fighting for each other's air.

168 | K BROMBERG

There is nothing gentle between us. Our movements are spurred on by a mixture of need and greed and desire and demand.

We bump heads and tables as we gasp for more. We scrape nails over bare skin and dig fingers into soft flesh. And it feels like fucking forever by the time I go get a condom and put it on, but the minute I do, we roll over one more time until Stevie is on top.

Her eyes meet mine as she rises up onto her knees, lines up my cock to her center, and then ever so slowly sinks down onto me.

It's the only time we slow down. The only time we feel like we're catching our breaths even though it feels like we stop breathing.

And then she begins to move. To ride me with a writhe of her hips and the press of her ass. She sinks her teeth into her bottom lip as her head falls back.

She's fucking gorgeous. With a flush to her cheeks. With some of her hair falling over her shoulder and onto her chest—but not enough, so her dark pink nipples peek through. With the feel of her wrapped around me, milking me with each and every movement.

She rocks over me, one hand exposing her clit while the other rubs it back and forth. She begins to move a little faster as her fingers speed up and she grows wetter.

I can see when her orgasm hits her. Every part of her tenses around me—thighs, pussy, hands—as she stills and a broken moan falls from her parted lips.

The sight of her, the feel of her, the sound of her . . . all three push and pull on everything inside of me until my breath is coming shorter, my hands are urging her hips harder, and my hips are pumping up into her.

"Stevie," I groan. It's all I can utter, all I can think of, as I empty myself.

She waits until we're both done before rolling off me and falling onto her back on the floor beside me with a thump and laughter.

"Mark off sex on a rug on the Cards O' Fun," she says with a giggle.

"*Cards O' Fun?*"

She sighs and I'd like to think it's from satisfaction, but the mischievous look in her eyes says differently. "It was a game that Vivi and Jordan made up . . ." She goes on to explain about the game. Dares and them giving her a chance to live it up. A competition she refused to lose.

And how it led her to me that first night.

"You're not saying anything," she says and pokes me in the ribs.

"Nothing to say. You were struggling with the loss of your father. Your friends were trying to pick you up. The antics and bad press that ensued may not have been the best route to take, but it is what it is. End of story." And *thank God* it was me they chose that night, or I'd have to kick some random guy's ass for touching her.

I shrug the thought away, distracted by her fingers still on my skin, as her comment comes back to me.

"Sex on the rug?" I ask.

"Yep. We had sex on the table. Now it's on the rug. I'm not very experienced, Finn, so I've got to note all these important firsts."

Her honesty strips me bare in the best and most surprising ways. It's not like we've talked about our past sex lives but for her to be inexperienced *and* be as secure in her sexuality as she is . . . it's a damn fucking turn-on.

"Important firsts will be noted from now on." I laugh.

"As they should be." She sighs. "I guess the bikini worked."

I start laughing. How can I not? I was blatantly and willingly seduced by a yellow bikini and an irresistible woman.

What has this world come to?

"I thought I was supposed to be the one fucking you hard and fast, though?" I ask, needing to say something, anything, to explain why that felt like way more than mindless fucking.

"You'll get your turn, Sanderson."

"*Ah yes*, the desk fantasy."

It's her turn to laugh.

It's my turn to hope.

Chapter

THIRTY-FOUR

Stevie

THE NIGHT BREEZE IS COOL AGAINST MY SKIN.

Finn's body is warm as I snuggle into him. My nose is under the curve of his jaw and I find an odd comfort in the scrape of his stubble every time his chest rises and falls.

His arms tighten around me, his breath even in my ear, and I relish the relaxing sounds of the ocean muted through the closed slider door.

I wake with a start, disoriented, and then flustered to look over and see that I'm not really in Finn's arms but more or less lying on the chaise section of the couch while he's sprawled out on the long side of it.

It all comes back to me now. The yellow bikini. The incredible sex. The things I said that now I'm blushing about. And the collapsing on the couch afterward where we talked about nothing of importance until we fell asleep—an easy way for us to avoid the awkward *I'm going to my bedroom* and *you're going to your bedroom* thing.

So, we lay on the couches, talking about anything and everything that was inconsequential until I fell asleep.

I turn to look at Finn and a small part of me sighs. The part that liked the feeling of my dream. The lying there together when I've never really slept with someone after sex, the feel of his heartbeat beneath my cheek, the subtle scent of the cologne on his skin.

It was just sex, Stevie. Just a dream. Stop your sleep-drugged thoughts about how nice it would be to wake up in his arms. The ones you were snuggling into a dream to. Go to your own bed.

I push myself up from the couch, my muscles sore from both practice and the rolling around on the floor with him, but then stop and study Finn.

He looks peaceful in his sleep. The intensity with which he seems to do everything in life is softened right now by the light of the moon. His chest rises and falls evenly, and I can't help but remember my dream. The peace and safety I felt snuggled up against him.

Just. Sex.

Then why as I stare at him do I feel like I . . . nothing. Never mind. The man helped me when I was in need of an escape. He helped provide it. Of course, that makes this bond between us more than just the sex, but . . . hell, we're good together.

I move to the wall of windows with the intention of looking out of it, but I can't seem to tear my eyes off Finn as I relive earlier.

A cat-ate-the-canary grin slides onto my lips.

There was power in the sex for me.

A sense of sexuality I don't think I've ever felt, and a confidence I don't think I've ever had before. Something about Finn made me comfortable enough to have it. To own it. His reactions, *God, his reactions* will live in my memory, because they were so goddamn sexy and arousing and powerful. To feel his legs trembling as I took him deep. To watch his heavy-lidded eyes darken as I talked dirty to him. To watch him come undone as I rocked back and forth over him. To hear my name on his lips and know that I did that to him.

I always thought Vivi and Jordan were full of shit when they said there was power in sex.

Now, I know better.

Now, I know what it's like to own your sexuality and I can't wait to own it again.

His words rumble through my head.

Important firsts will be noted from now on.

From now on . . .

I give in to the want and move toward him, pressing a soft kiss to his lips. A type of thank-you for whatever therapy of his this is.

Because he is helping me. In some way. Somehow.

He is definitely a balm to the damaged parts of me. *And he's proud of me.* That's something my dad used to say to me too. And even that gives me confidence, because Finn's opinion matters.

I give him one last look before I head toward the hallway and push away the thought hinting in my mind.

The one that says our time is limited . . . so I need to enjoy it while it lasts.

Chapter
THIRTY-FIVE

Stevie

"You sound better. More settled," Vivi says.

"I am. *I think.*" My laugh fills the line and hits my own ears but I like how it sounds. Genuine instead of on the edge of hysteria as it had been. "Definitely better."

"Is it the tennis you're practicing, the interview you gave, or the man you're staying with who's helping foster that?" she asks, curiosity edging her tone.

I think for a beat. "Maybe it's all three."

"Honesty." She sounds surprised. "I'm impressed."

"Gee. Thanks." I laugh again, and God, does it feel good.

"No, I just mean, we knew it was hard for you, losing your dad. We knew you weren't ready to talk about it. Or the future. So, we kind of let you get lost in the outside for a bit to help quiet the noise, if that makes sense. We tried to challenge you with things to push you outside of your box to prevent you from breaking down . . . but maybe we were wrong. Maybe that's what you needed in order to get to this stage you're at now."

I know what she means by that. Now. And I also know that when I was with them, I didn't feel quite as alone as I had when Dad first passed. They'd come when I'd asked though, and I knew I was . . . *am* so lucky to have friends who do that.

"Who knew what I needed . . . but thank you for being there for me regardless."

"Always. You know that. We had your back then, and we have your back now."

Chapter
THIRTY-SIX

Stevie

"Kellen," I groan as I plop down on the bench, exhausted, and drenched with sweat. "You're relentless."

"And that's how you like me," Kellen says. The smile he throws my way is smug as he picks up some of the balls on the court.

"Huh."

"Enjoy this weather here—this California sunshine and cool coastal breeze—because when we get to New York in a few weeks, it's going to be miserable. Muggy and hot to the point that it smothers you."

"Don't remind me." I wipe my face with the towel. "And the crappy part? The crappy part is I haven't even gotten to explore anywhere here because I've been locked up tight."

"Should we start calling you Rapunzel?"

I whip my head over to see Finn standing on the side of the court, his arms crossed over his chest, his sunglasses on. Is it ridiculous that my heart jumps at the sound of his voice and the sight of him even though I see him every day?

Kellen laughs. "I could think of a lot of things to call her, but Rapunzel ain't one of them."

"Funny." I raise my middle finger at him but laugh while doing it before standing and moving toward Finn. "What are you doing here?"

It's been two days since the sex on the floor. He's been busy. I've been busy. Or maybe if I'm honest with myself, I've been kind of lying low because I was uncertain how this dynamic between us would go.

But he's here when I know he's knee-deep in a serious contract nego-tiation as well as fixing some problems a client got himself in. Problems that I have a feeling he normally would tend to in person but has chosen to do remotely instead.

Because of me.

Finn shrugs and his smile widens. "I figured you've been training here for a few weeks and I've yet to see how it's going for myself, so . . ."

"So as a good agent would, you decided to mosey the quarter of a mile from your house and come see me."

"Something like that," he murmurs and I stare at him from beneath my visor, my own smile wide, wishing I could see his eyes.

"So did you like what you saw?"

"I did." He nods. "*I do.*"

I mock curtsy and laugh. "And?"

"And, *Rapunzel*, after seeing the crude art you left on the kitchen table with the silverware," he says, "I realized you might be getting a lit-tle stir-crazy."

"Just a little." I hold my thumb and index finger about an inch apart, a small thrill shooting through me at the prospect of getting out of the house. Not to mention I love that he saw my message and understood its meaning. "Was the SOS I created too obvious?"

"Perhaps."

"Do you know how hard it is to use silverware to spell?"

He laughs. "Maybe I was feeling slightly the same."

"So what are we going to do about it?"

"I'm rescuing you from the tower, Rapunzel. It's time to let your hair down."

Chapter
THIRTY-SEVEN

Finn

"I'm more than impressed that you even knew the story of Rapunzel to begin with," Stevie says, the warm glow of the candlelight reflecting off her tan skin and dancing in her eyes.

The second-story outdoor patio is quiet tonight. A frequent favorite when I'm in town, I asked the owner if I could have the private balcony to myself tonight, and luckily it was available. The small area sits above the main restaurant, so that we can see other diners but they can't see us.

Lights are strung back and forth over the terracotta tiled floor adding warmth to the atmosphere. Dishes clink and glasses clank while a mariachi band plays quietly in the corner of the main floor.

"It's my favorite of the Disney movies."

She lifts her brows. "You have a favorite Disney movie?"

"Well, let me correct that comment. When I'm forced to watch Disney movies with my cousins' kids, that's the one I'm partial to."

Her smile widens. "Even that surprises me. You seem like a man who no one forces to do anything."

Except for meeting you. That first meeting in Carson's suite flashes through my mind.

"For the most part." He shrugs. "Besides, the hero's name is Flynn Rider so I figure it's close enough to assume they were writing about me..."

"Oh Jesus." She barks out a laugh. "Ego much?"

"Flynn. Finn. Close enough for me," I tease.

She shakes her head with an adorable smile on her lips and asks, "Do you have a big family?"

"No. I mostly know my dad's side of it, hence the cousins."

"What's your dad like?"

My sigh is heavy. "Like someone I never want to be like."

"Oh. I'm sorry. I didn't mean to—"

"You're fine. It is what it is. My mom leaving turned him into a bitter man who wanted to make his son be the same."

"So you don't see him much?"

"He died of a heart attack years ago."

"I'm sorry."

"Don't be. He wasn't exactly the nicest man. Never a kind or supportive word, something I didn't realize until I worked with Carson for a while, actually. After my mom left, he took any and every opportunity to push his agenda. Tough love wasn't even on his radar. As I said, bitter."

"Well, if it's worth noting, he failed. His son isn't bitter. His son is successful and polite albeit demanding at times, and good at *many* things."

"Should my ego swell with pride at that last part?" I ask, wanting my father nowhere near whatever this is with Stevie.

"No complaints here."

I lean back in my chair, my elbows on the armrests, and a margarita in my hand as I angle my head and stare at her.

We've been here for almost an hour, and it's been . . . effortless. Normally on a date, I don't care much for the conversation. *I haven't cared* about the conversation. Women have been there for my purposes alone, and at the end of the night, once I've pleasured them and got what I needed, I've sent them on their way. I've kept them at arm's length, never wanting anything else. I've kept my father's words foremost in my heart— *that women are nothing more than a distraction, who will play you and screw you over*—even though the man was filled with resentment and misery.

And yet I care about what this woman says, someone I should consider completely off limits both because she's my client and nearly a decade younger than me. *Why?* What made her the woman I see in front of me?

"*Who are you*, Stevie Lancaster?" I don't mean to put words to my thoughts but they're out before I can stop them.

"I'm just a girl who likes the simple things most days and the roar of a crowd on others."

"Do you like it? The crowd?"

Stevie sits back, her eyes watching her fingers trace around the rim of her glass before meeting my eyes. "It's what I do and all I know. I mean, I've been doing this, competing professionally and training, for ten years."

"But do you still love it? The fanfare, the competition, the crowds?"

A smile ghosts her lips and tears mist in her eyes. "It's a rush and if anyone tells you differently, they're lying. But it's also like being in a pressure cooker that can either explode because the lid isn't screwed on properly or it can create the most perfect meal." She snorts and places a hand to the middle of her face like a little girl would. "That was the lamest thing I've ever said. Oh my God, I'm such a dork."

"I just told you I had a favorite Disney movie so I'm pretty sure I already took that title."

"I think we're tied." She holds her glass out to mine and I tap mine against it. "Cheers."

"What are we toasting to?" I ask.

"To tonight." She stands abruptly as the music changes from traditional mariachi to a slow, sultry Santana song. "Dance with me, Finn."

She moves around the patio, closing her eyes and swinging her hips to the beat as if she doesn't have a care in the world.

I can't take my eyes off her. I wouldn't want to if I could.

It was so much easier having a damaged Stevie than the one dancing hypnotically in front of me. Damaged had me stepping back and putting the brakes on any and all lust. Damaged put me in check so I didn't want her more. So I wouldn't hurt her further.

Then she figured her shit out. She did it on her own and it made her all the more attractive because of it.

And now she's standing there, her fingers waving to me to come to her, and I'm fucking useless at resisting.

"C'mon, Finn. Let loose with me."

"I'm not good at dancing," I warn, but my feet move toward her.

"I'm not good at a lot of things, but I do them anyway."

The music continues and then she's in my arms. Her body sways against mine. Her lips meet mine.

And tonight, everything just feels that *easy.*

The thought is almost comical after you consider the first week that we met, but it is.

The conversation.

The comfortable silence.

The wanting—*her*—every minute of every goddamn day.

Chapter
THIRTY-EIGHT

Stevie

I watch Finn from the doorway of his office.

God knows what time it is, but the buzz of my margarita and the high from the sex we had when we got home has faded with the early morning hour.

He looks just as tired as I feel as he sits behind his desk in nothing but a pair of board shorts and some seriously mussed-up hair.

Yet he works, and I silently watch.

The man tugs on things inside of me. Wires. Strings. Last nerves. But I've laughed more than I can remember as of late. I've wanted to feel instead of wanting to feel numb.

I'm proud of you.

Those four words have rung in my ears far longer than they should and yet, they meant more to me than he ever could have known.

"Hey, what are you doing up?" he asks, startling when he sees me standing there before turning his chair to face me.

"Can't sleep."

"Are you telling me I didn't do my job properly?" His sleep-drugged smile flips my stomach over.

I step into the room. "No complaints here." He definitely tired me out in the physical sense, but my mind won't shut off.

"But something is bugging you." Instead of answering, I move into the room and rest my hips on the desk beside where he sits. "What is it, Stevie?"

"I was afraid to ask earlier but now I can't stop wondering."

"Ask what?"

"*About her.*" He raises his eyebrows at my comment. "I deleted all social media off my phone so that I don't get distracted from training. After my interview last week, has she done more press? Has she gotten more attention? Is she still out there?"

Finn reaches out and puts a hand on my hip. "She tried to the first day or two after, but your interview pretty much put water on her fire. The only people willing to give her the time of day are the same magazines who have cover stories about how an alien impregnated a seven-foot-tall woman so . . . yeah, everything pretty much lost steam after your interview."

"At least I did something right," I murmur as I pick at the edges of my nail polish.

"Hey?" he asks, his hand shaking my hip. "What else is going on?"

I twist my lips as guilt eats at me. "I thought I was going to regret saying some of the things I said in the interview. That I was going to regret my decision to not talk to her, but other than hoping I'm nothing like her, I haven't questioned it at all."

"Then you made the right decision."

I stand there hearing his words and know he understands better than anyone. "Sorry. I'll let you get back to work. You must be exhausted."

"I'm so tired, I can't even see straight," he says and laughs before he does something completely unexpected when he rolls his chair over in front of me and rests his forehead against my stomach. His sigh is heavy, and for the first time, I realize just how much Finn has given up or put aside by bringing me here.

He has a full client list to tend to—some he probably needs to visit in person—and yet he's here, tending to me. Making sure no one finds out my whereabouts. Giving me the space and time to live my life without the cameras in my face—something I asked for when he first brought me here.

"You need an assistant," I say.

"I have an assistant. And an intern and a secretary . . . I have a whole office full of people in Manhattan but it's me who people want to deal with so that makes it hard to not answer the calls."

Guilt eats at me for taking him away from that—his life, his work, his routine—and yet I can't imagine being here without him.

"I understand that. And it makes you who you are." I run my fingers through his hair, rubbing his scalp to try and help him relax.

He grunts in response.

"What's your real name?" I ask out of the blue.

"Huh?"

"Is Finn short for something?"

"Why?"

"I don't know. It's one of those dorky two-in-the-morning questions that float through my mind."

"Finnegan Alexander Sanderson."

"That suits you." And I'm not sure why I care to know, but I repeat it in my head, over and over, almost as if it's something I might forget when our time here is done.

He shrugs, and I chuckle when something tucked in the corner of his desk plotter catches my eye.

Have a one-night stand.

"How did you get that?" I ask, completely stunned that he has it.

"Get what?" Finn asks lifting his head.

"My Cards O' Fun card."

"It was on the hallway floor. It must have dropped out of your suitcase when you were getting your stuff," he says resting his forehead back against me. "I thought it was funny so I kept it."

"Funny?"

"Yeah, it's how we first met, isn't it?" he asks rhetorically. "You took the dare. You met me. And here we are." He shrugs. "You're not mad, are you?"

Because he can't see me, he misses the cheesy grin on my face. "No. Not at all."

And even minutes later when I snuggle in on the couch in his office, the click of his fingers on his keyboard as he keeps working lulling me to sleep, that cheesy grin is still there, still plastered on my lips.

What does it mean if you find a guy who keeps a sentimental token of what might be called your disastrous first date? Some might say a keeper, but this is Finn. *Finnegan Alexander Sanderson.* And something tells me that Finn isn't a man who wants to be kept.

Chapter
THIRTY-NINE

Finn

SEX IS A WEIRD THING.

It's awesome obviously, but it's also weird.

Like when you're seeing someone, you have sex, and then have a valid excuse to leave. Like your own house. Your own life. It allows you to get a break from the person. You don't answer the phone if you don't want to talk. You don't respond to texts if you're afraid that you're going to get sick of them too soon.

It connects you but then can also drive you apart. Sometimes you use it to do that on purpose.

Or at least I have.

So how are you supposed to handle the person when you're living with them?

Even more so, what if that person is living with you, having sex with you, spending more time with you than you've ever spent with someone before, and you still aren't sick of them? What the fuck does that mean?

That's been my train of thought as I take a long jog on the beach to clear my head.

My conclusion?

Does it fucking matter? I've slept with her to try and get over her. That clearly didn't work.

Now I'm sleeping with her knowing she'll leave for the Open and then that will be that. Fling over. Time well spent. Mind-blowing sex had.

Stop fucking overthinking everything and just go with it.

So why am I picking up my pace to make sure I'm back at the house for when she gets home?

I jog down the street and purposely pretend to look at my watch as I move past Kristen's house, ignoring her just like I've ignored the numerous texts she's sent over the past few weeks.

I'm sure she's more than curious who the woman was in my house. I'm even more certain the SUV with the dark, tinted windows, which pulls out from behind my gate every morning and arrives back every evening with Stevie inside, has Kristen even more desperate to understand why I'm ignoring her.

By the same token, I've let numerous clients use my house over the years so the neighbors should be used to the blacked-out windows and secrecy.

The only difference is I've been here the whole time too.

I punch in the gate code, my phone already in hand as I begin scrolling through the emails that have come in since I started my workout. One after another after another. Some bullshit. Some simply noise. Very few are pressing.

At least I'll have the evening off, and then my mind goes to Stevie and what trouble we can get ourselves into.

Not a bad way to spend an evening.

And isn't that funny? A few weeks ago, I'd consider a night alone with one woman, in my house no less, to be a sign of the apocalypse.

That's not how I spend my nights. Typically, they involve my laptop, a glass of expensive whiskey, and maybe a game on TV. Other nights involve a woman, some time between her thighs, and then an excuse to leave.

But never this.

Never me looking forward to how I'm going to relax at home with a woman. In my house. Without being able to bail after having sex.

Not a bad way to spend an evening.

Christ.

The house smells like Faith has been baking and no man would ever complain about that prospect. But as I turn the corner to enter the kitchen, I'm knocked off my stride when I see Stevie standing there with flour dusting her shoulder, her face etched in concentration, a smear of what looks like frosting on her cheek, and her tongue between her teeth as she tries to cut the top off what looks to be a layer of uniced cake.

"Should I be worried that you're baking?" I ask remembering a conversation we had somewhere about the severe limitations on her culinary skills.

Her head whips up—eyes wide and smile shy—and I swear to God my fucking heart stops. That's the only way I can describe what that constricting feeling in my chest is when her eyes meet mine.

"You're not supposed to be home yet," she says, obviously flustered, the knife stopping halfway through the top of the cake.

"I wasn't aware I had a schedule." I take a step closer, still staring at her, still trying to figure out why seeing her like this is striking a chord with me in the most foreign of ways.

"We have a schedule," she says matter-of-factly and then makes a squeaking noise when something she's doing goes wrong. Her expression is adorable as she tries to fix whatever she's trying to fix before she glances up at me. "You go to work. I go to training. Then we meet back here in the kitchen in about thirty minutes to talk about our days." She points to the clock. "You're early."

I laugh. "Okay. But what am I early for?"

She innocently licks what appears to be frosting off her fingers and I don't think I've ever wanted to be frosting so bad in my life.

"I was attempting to make you a cake."

"A cake?"

"A carrot cake with homemade cream cheese frosting, in fact."

The surprises keep getting even better.

I step up to the counter and survey the damage. It looks nothing like the perfectly frosted carrot cakes that Faith has made me in the past. There are two round layers cut horribly askew, one is frosted with the crumbs all mixed in so the white frosting looks like dirt is peeking through. The frosting is in a bowl, but it has lumps and bumps with powdered sugar thrown all over the counter from where she lifted the mixer up from the bowl. There are carrots half peeled on the far end and a half-melted stick of butter on the other.

It's a fucking disaster, but it's the most awesome fucking disaster I've ever seen.

She tried to bake me my favorite cake.

"It looks . . ."

"Like a disaster." She chuckles the words out as she steps backward and takes in the whole mess.

But all I see is her in the moment. The messy hair. The disappointment that it doesn't look better. The pride that it looks as good as it does. A woman trying to do something for me when I expect nothing.

I reach a finger out and swipe it in the frosting and lick it off. "Damn. That's good."

"It is?"

The hope in her voice, in her smile, in her eyes fucking undoes me. My mouth is on hers in an instant. She tastes like frosting and desire and everything I suddenly seem to want, every second of every damn day.

My hands are in her hair. On her hips. Lifting her up so that her ass is on the counter and she's at the same height as me.

Yes, my dick's hard already (when is it not when it comes to Stevie?) but there's something about her kiss that consumes me completely. That makes me want to enjoy the moment in a way we haven't before.

There's hunger in our kiss, a sated desperation, but underlying that is a desire to savor it. To take our time. To enjoy the moment.

We've never done this. Slowed down. Not gone from the starting point to the end game and maybe, I want to put the end game on hold for a moment. Maybe I want to enjoy Stevie and her kiss.

And when it's over, I rest my forehead against hers, still trying to figure out what that pressure in my chest is.

"Well, wow. If that's what I get when I bake you a shitty cake, I wonder how I'd be rewarded if I made you something that actually looked good."

I lean back and look at her, a half-cocked smile on my lips, my thumb reaching out to dust some flour off the side of her chin. "Why all of this trouble?"

"Happy birthday," she whispers with a sheepish shrug.

I blink several times at her, more than aware that it's not my birthday, but the last thing I want to do is hurt her feelings, especially when she went to so much trouble.

"I—"

"I know it's not your real birthday," she explains. "I mean, I wish it were though because then this would all be easier."

"You lost me." I chuckle and take another lick of frosting.

"I wanted to do something nice for you. I was fishing for a reason to celebrate something so I could make you your favorite. I asked Faith when your birthday was. She said it was at the end of next month and since I'm not going to be here then"—she clears her throat and I wonder if those words, that thought, bugs her as much as it does me—"I thought we could celebrate it now. *Tonight.*"

"Tonight?"

"Yep." She gives a resolute nod.

"You're serious?"

"Does your kitchen look like I'm serious?"

I laugh and just shake my head at her. "Take that, Cards O' Fun," I murmur and smother her laugh with my lips.

Chapter
FORTY

Stevie

"So when are you coming *home?*" Vivi whines and pouts across the Zoom connection.

"I'm thinking after the Open. I have three weeks left here, then the Open, so . . . four or five weeks." I take a sip of my wine and lean back on my headboard, more than happy to see her face.

"We'd offer to come and cheer for you at the tournament, but I think big-shot agent man would draw the line."

"Well, big-shot agent man doesn't own me." I chuckle at the nickname.

"He may not own you, but he sure as hell has you twisted up in knots." A smug smile spreads on her lips as she stares at me, daring me to refute her.

"Whatever," I play it off. "He does not."

"Are you forgetting the fact that I know you, Stevie Lancaster? I know that you avoid me when you don't want to tell me the truth, and girl, my texts have been going unanswered for days on end." She lifts her eyebrows and just stares at me. "There is no shame in finishing what you started that first night you met, but it seems since then, the two of you have made your own Cards O' Fun to live out."

I fight my smile and give in with a shrug. "Perhaps."

"Ahh," she murmurs and studies me longer.

"So, you're living in his house, training nearby, and living the quiet life all while sleeping with him in between the day-to-day stuff, right?"

My mind immediately shifts to highlight reels of the past few days.

My horrible carrot cake with its layer that slid off the other, and how he laughed when I brought him the candlelit disaster. Of the sex in his shower that was full of soapy hands and delicious kisses. Of the stolen kiss on the patio this morning before he took a conference call. Of how I caught him looking at me across the room the other day with a soft smile.

"Something like that," I finally answer.

"And when the Open comes, you're going to be perfectly fine just walking away from the built-in sex and the seeing each other every day that you've grown accustomed to?"

I take a sip of wine to buy myself the time to answer. Finn's voice booms down the hallway through my closed door as he talks on the phone with a client about something. Will I miss that constant reminder of his presence even though we aren't actually interacting with each other? Will I hear him humming as he does every morning when that first sip of coffee hits his tongue? Will I fall asleep on couches from now on because it's easier for us to do that than to broach the subject of how we can have sex together but aren't sure if we should sleep in the same bed?

"I'm waiting while you're stalling."

I laugh, loving her, missing her, and hating how well she knows me all at the same time. "We're just enjoying the time we have."

"So that means neither of you have really talked about it." She gives a dramatic eye roll.

"That means why talk about it when it's not going to change anything? I'm here to train, then I'll move on with my life. He's kind of put his life on hold and he has to get back to it. It is what it is."

"Mm-hmm." She stares at me through the screen and I all but squirm in my seat. "Tell me, after you two get down to it, where do you sleep?"

"What do you mean, where do we sleep?"

"I mean, are you falling asleep in his bed or are you in your bed or . . . where?"

I laugh nervously. "We don't really make it to either bed. We kind of have a habit of having sex in different places."

"Different places?" she asks because now I definitely have her attention.

"The couch. Outside on the deck. The floor. The shower. You know, *places.*"

I've got to note all these important firsts . . .

And oh, how we've noted them. This time I don't fight the grin but just stare right back at her with one eyebrow raised.

"Humph. Then maybe you're right. Maybe this is just a thing between you. A man will only let you fall asleep in his bed if shit's getting serious."

"Thank you, oh wise relationship counselor," I say with every ounce of sarcasm I have.

"At your service." She mock bows. "But seriously, he's treating you right? Because there was a while there where I wasn't sure if he was a bastard or—"

"He'll tell you himself he's a bastard," I murmur, "but it's all a lie. He's really a great guy."

The thought echoes through my head long after Vivi ends our video chat. Her words, her questions, ride shotgun right beside it and I wonder if it's something we should address—how this ends.

I'm pretty sure I'm scared to ask because I already know the answer.

This is sex. This is just sex.

It's become the words we utter every single time we have it. Kind of like our mantra so we each understand what this is, so that neither of us thinks otherwise.

But I wonder if I say it and he repeats it because it's what he wants or because he thinks it's what I want.

I wonder what would happen if it wasn't said at all.

With my glass of wine in hand, I stroll through the darkened house. A few lights are on in the kitchen and the breeze floating through the family room tells me the windows are open, and that's where I'll find Finn.

He makes a striking figure where he stands at the railing. There is tension in his shoulders, and I wonder what athlete or organization is causing troubles today.

"Want to talk about it?" I ask as I walk up beside him.

"Is it that noticeable?"

"You always come out here, stand at the railing, and stare at the ocean when you're stressed about something."

"Huh," he says. "I didn't realize I was that predictable."

"I wonder what it is you do when you're in Manhattan when you're stressed."

"I sit with a whiskey in a chair and look at the city moving nonstop below."

And I can picture it. His empty condo behind him decorated in dark hues much like this house is. Finn sunk down into a stuffed leather couch with his head leaning back, his shirt unbuttoned some, and a glass of whiskey dangling from his fingers.

I suddenly feel a pang of longing to see that in person, but I shake it away as soon as I realize what it is.

"So what did your client do this time?"

"It's what I can't do for him. I can't make him better than he is. I can't make him want to be better. I can't wipe his attitude away so that teams want him. I can't control the uncontrollable while he can and yet, he just thinks I'm trying to tell him what to do and disrespect him." He blows out a long breath.

"He sounds like he has a chip on his shoulder."

He snorts and nods. "I recruited him out of high school. I promised his mom and dad that I was going to do everything I could to help him reach the top. I even thought up a stupid little thing he used to do before every game when the cameras were on him." Finn lifts his hand and pats it three times over his heart. "It was his way of saying he loved them and that he missed them." His smile is reticent. "I told them I would take care of their son, but I lied. I can't do anything more and that broken promise weighs heavily on me."

"Shh. Your secret is safe with me."

He looks over at me and for the first time, I see the bags under his eyes and notice how tired he is. "What secret?"

"That Finn Sanderson has a huge heart." I press a kiss to his shoulder. "You found a way to keep hope within the hearts of a boy's parents. You could have told him to forget about them and focus all his attention on what you tell him. But you showed him that hearts matter. That his parents' love mattered. That knowing someone loves you matters." That's rare and precious. *Finn understands what love is.*

He emits a half-hearted laugh but it's his expression that has me staring longer. "I think you have me mixed up with another guy."

"Nope. I've seen it with my own eyes. From how you treated me—"

"You know that first meeting with Carson I was ready to throw you over the balcony, right?"

"To how dedicated you are with your clients."

"Most of them drive me crazy at some point," he mutters.

"To how you're working more, not traveling like you usually do because of me."

"That's minor."

"No, it's not. It's huge . . . to me."

Finn angles his head to the side and stares at me in the same way he did in the kitchen the other day. It's unnerving in the best of ways, and I give in to the urge to step up and press a tender kiss on his lips.

"Like I said," I murmur. "Your secret is safe with me."

A cheer goes up on the beach down below that startles the two of us apart. There is a camera flash that lights up the night sky and Finn immediately pushes me behind him.

The paparazzi have found me.

My heart falls, thinking my time of anonymity is up. That the freedom I've had here is now gone.

"Christ," he mutters as he leans to look over the railing just as another flash goes off followed by a round of oohs and aahs.

Finn stills at the sound at the same time I look around him and see it.

"Look!" he shouts to the waves down below. As they hit the shore, the white froth turns an iridescent, bright neon blue.

"Oh my God." I step out from behind him, realizing that each wave makes the water glow even more. It's beautiful. It's crazy. *It's incredible.* "*What is that?*"

"I've heard of it," he says, holding his hand out to me as he starts to move down the stairs to the beach, "but have never been here when it happens. It's called . . ." He quiets while he tries to remember the word. "Bioluminescence."

My laugh cuts through the night. "You say that like I'm supposed to know what it means."

"It's the plankton blooming or something like that. It lights up the water."

We have sand beneath our toes in seconds and move away from the pockets of people watching the spectacle on the beach. The dark night sky allows me to keep my anonymity.

But I don't think anyone is looking at me as Mother Nature continues to display her brilliance with each crash of the waves.

"Look," Finn says as he drags his toes through the wet sand and it streaks with the blue light.

Like a little kid, I follow suit and begin dragging my feet every few steps so I can do the same. Then the digging of our toes leads to kicking water on each other so that our shirts start glowing with the splashed water.

Finn's laughter rumbles through the night air as we chase each other like little kids on the beach. I shriek when he hits me with a huge kick of water that soaks my whole back. Chills chase over my skin from the cold water. He taunts me and then takes off. I follow suit, knowing damn well I can outrun him.

The past five weeks have done wonders for my speed and stamina and it shows when I chase him down and grab his shirt from behind. We both laugh as we tumble and then yelp when we're met with the cold of the water.

We both come up out of breath and sputtering with the water glowing surrounding us. I run a hand through the water at my hips and it looks like lightning is striking underwater, as the neon streaks in the path I just made through the water.

"This is so cool," I say, mesmerized by something I never knew existed before tonight.

"It is, isn't it?" Finn asks as he grabs my hand to help me from the water.

"Look." I point to his wet shirt that's now glowing from where it came in contact with the water. "Not only do you have a heart, but now it's glowing."

He watches as I pat over his heart three times, much like he said his client did, and stares at the blue fading beneath my fingers. "Who knew? That might come as a huge shock to a lot of people." He chuckles while averting his eyes from mine, seemingly uncomfortable in the moment.

"It's not a shock to me," I whisper.

His gaze meets mine this time. Emotions swim in his eyes that I can't exactly decipher. Or maybe I can because they look how I feel, and I'm not one hundred percent certain I can admit to any of it yet.

Perhaps he can't either.

Finn's lips meet mine in the most tender of kisses, right where we're standing in the water with people all around us. His hands glow as they frame my face and we get lost in each other as if no one is around.

There's a fluttering in my belly.

A deep-seated need that somehow feels like it's being satisfied while at the same time being enhanced.

It's unlike anything I've ever felt before.

A kiss is just a kiss and yet this moment—his lips, his touch, the uniqueness of the glowing water—makes it feel like so much more.

And even as the thought ebbs and flows through my mind, I know the way I feel has nothing to do with the water.

It has to do with him. Finn.

He's made it so that feeling isn't a bad thing anymore. I've spent months trying not to and in this short amount of time, he makes me look forward to the time I get to spend with him because he makes me feel good. Great. Like I'm floating on air.

And when we get back to the house and strip off our soaking-wet clothes, we get lost in each other all over again.

Chapter
FORTY-ONE

Stevie

DAYS RUN TOGETHER.

Ones filled with training and then laughter. With quick glances and the sudden awareness that our days are numbered.

In the past, I've only had to worry about tournaments. About being ready and prepping as best as I can. But now? Now there is an added element that I'm not sure whether I love or hate. *I'm going to miss this.*

Being here.

Having a place that feels like home.

Him.

I pull my floppy sun hat down lower on my head as I pass a couple on the beach, needing to keep this anonymity as long as I can before I hit the bright lights and powder keg of stress at the Open. It's been heaven having anonymity. Being able to practice without a gaggle of people standing outside that I have to fight my way through. Being able to work on something with Kellen without fearing an article will be printed saying I'm off my game because I keep repeating the same strokes over and over.

I can't remember the last time I was afforded this type of freedom.

"There you are."

I turn at the sound of Finn's voice. "What are you doing down here?"

He grabs my hand and links his fingers with mine. "Taking a walk with you."

"But you said you have a list a mile long to get done today."

"I did. I do." He shrugs and looks over to where a bunch of kids are digging in the sand and throwing it at each other. "But I looked out the window and saw you down here in this very sexy hat"—he reaches out with his free hand and tugs on it— "and I figured that work could wait and a walk with a beautiful woman couldn't."

Is it silly that my stomach flutters at his words? That I'm flattered he took a pause from his work to come down here and spend time with me? Is it even sillier that my cheeks hurt from smiling so hard that he did?

This man makes me feel good. About myself. About my future. About the day-to-day. I've never experienced that before.

Sure, I had my dad there day in, day out, pushing me to be an incredible tennis player.

But it's almost like Finn has been here day in and day out, showing me what it feels like to be a woman. With his words and his actions and the glances across the room.

"Oh, you make my heart go pitter-patter," I tease to cover my sudden inability to speak.

He just squeezes my hand and swings them as we keep walking. The silence is comfortable between us, not forced or awkward, and yet there is a weight to it.

"What is it, Sanderson? You're silent but you've got a lot to say."

He chuckles. "You leave in ten days."

And there it is. What we've been avoiding. What we have kissed and slept our way around without actually saying out loud.

"I do." I give a measured nod.

"Do you think that you're ready?"

For the briefest of seconds, my heart falls. I thought he was talking about me going because he was going to miss me, not because his agent hat is on and he's thinking about me professionally.

I clear my throat of the sudden emotion swelling there and nod to give myself a second. "Yes. I do. I think I'll be able to compete."

"I think you'd be able to compete even if you hadn't been training as hard as you have been. That's just you."

"It is." I give a soft smile and steal a glance at him from beneath my hat before looking back at the sand in front of us. "But I think I will be able to perform well, meaning I'm going in there confident in where I'm at."

He nods but doesn't speak for another beat. "I'm going to miss you."

Tears well in my eyes for some reason and I'm not quite sure what to do with this odd sensation in my chest. "Me too."

Tell me you wish I could stay.

Tell me you want to make this work somehow.

Tell me something, *anything*, that expresses how you feel when you look at me.

"It's been a fun run, hasn't it?"

I laugh to release the sudden nerves racing through me. "It has. After we got off to a rocky start."

"And then there was the infamous strip poker incident—"

"—very funny—"

"—but I think we've more than made up for it."

"We have." My smile is bittersweet, sad even. I feel like we're choosing our words cautiously.

Because he's not going to tell me he wants me to stay.

Because he doesn't want this to work somehow.

Because he can't tell me something, anything, that expresses how he feels when he looks at me.

And this is why I should be telling myself things like "Didn't we both know this was going to come to an end?" Because *that* is our truth. That *is* our reality.

Knowing it would end and actually acknowledging it are two different things.

"Look." He stops to pick up a small, white sand dollar and turns it over in his hand before handing it to me. "For good luck."

"Thank you." I stare at the intricate designs on the delicate urchin and hate that tears blur my eyes.

Good luck at the Open.

Good luck in your life.

Good luck . . . because this is almost over.

"So what's next for you? Do you play the Open and then head back to Florida or will you immediately start training for the next tournament?"

"I'm not quite sure." *Because my dad used to tell me what was next.* "I've been so focused on the Open and getting there that I haven't really thought about the next steps." I shrug. *I haven't wanted to think of anything after the Open, because that hurts too much.* "Normally my dad determined where I'd head next, and it was often back home after the Open. So . . ." *Don't get teary, Stevie. Hold it together.* "I need to sort through my dad's things and handle all of that stuff. Maybe look at getting a new place."

"Do you think you're ready to?"

"Ready to what?"

"Sort through his things."

"I don't think anyone is ever ready to, but I'm in a much better headspace now to do so thanks to you."

"I didn't do anything, Stevie. You figured it all out on your own."

"I bet you'll be happy to get rid of me. To have your space back to yourself. To head back to your place in Manhattan. To be able to fly off and see clients at the drop of a dime when needed without worrying a certain female con artist is going to rob you blind." Finn doesn't laugh like I expect him to.

He doesn't even answer. Instead, he tucks me in close, his arm around my shoulder, my arms sliding around his waist, and we stare out at the water in silence.

My thoughts race and my heart feels heavy. This wasn't supposed to happen. I wasn't supposed to like Finn Sanderson let alone slowly fall in love with him.

Because isn't that what I've done?

Isn't that why I'm so upset right now?

Isn't that why I'm dreading what will happen in ten days?

"Why do I feel like we're already starting to say goodbye?" I finally ask.

"We're not. We're just forcing ourselves to get used to the idea." He tilts my chin up with his thumb and forefinger so that I'm forced to meet his eyes. There is emotion swimming in his eyes that matches how I feel. Confused. Worried. Sad. Missing me already. "But for now, we stay focused on your preparation for the Open, okay? You have had a tough one, Stevie, so let's keep taking each day as we are, staying focused on getting you another Grand Slam victory." He gives me a tight smile and then leans down to brush his lips against mine.

"Another victory." I clear my throat. "That's what Dad would want," I whisper. He smiles at me, and it's with such tenderness that tears form.

"Yes, that's what your dad would want," Finn says quietly.

But what I want is to get lost in Finn. Yes, I want victory at the Open, but I'm beginning to see that I want a win in another area of my life. And right now, that's more with Finn. *More.*

Chapter
FORTY-TWO

Finn

THERE HAS BEEN A SOMBER TONE TO THE HOUSE SINCE OUR WALK ON the beach. A sense that we know what's going to happen, don't want it to happen, but also the eagerness to get back to the lives we used to know.

So I work. Because not working, joining her on the beach for a walk or hearing her laugh or watching her as she plays those silly games on her phone with her bottom lip between her teeth, is a constant reminder that she's going to be gone soon.

If she wanted more, she'd tell me, right?

Fuck if I know.

Hell, I don't even want more.

You're such a fucking liar, Sanderson. You want more. You want a lot of fucking things when it comes to Stevie Lancaster but none of them are feasible.

Christ.

I welcome the buzzing of my phone. A client to help drown out the constant fucking noise in my head that goes against everything I've ever been told. That I've ever thought.

"Hey, Rowdy. What's up?"

Rowdy begins to talk. And talk. And talk. About the things he's being denied. About how he's being disrespected by not getting more playing time. About what justifies the huge chip on his shoulder that I know is turning his general manager and coach off.

But I know better than to speak up. I know I'm his sounding board so that he gets it off his chest instead of going off on his bosses.

"Hold on, let me put you on speaker because my phone is dying," I lie. But I know the way Rowdy talks, and my phone could die by the time he's done. "Okay. You're good."

His voice floods the room as I rise from my chair and move about my office, prepared for the long haul in this conversation. I look to see what's happening on the beach. I turn to fiddle with a few things on the bookshelf behind my desk. But it's only when I turn back to take a seat that I'm met with pure fucking perfection.

Stevie wasn't joking about that fantasy of hers because here she is, naked as can be, with her ass on my desk and her thighs spread. I'm not sure what I want to look at more, the goddamn perfection of her pussy or the smug seduction in her eyes.

"Are you hearing me, Sanderson?" Rowdy asks.

"I am," I say not having heard a single word he's said since seeing Stevie.

"Good. I'm not finished. I . . ."

He drones on, but I push mute on the speaker before acting on my one and only thought. *Tasting her*. I drop to my knees without saying a word and slide my tongue between her perfectly pink lips.

Her gasp, the way her one hand fists immediately in my hair, the way she tastes . . . is the hottest fucking turn-on.

Her thighs tense against my hands spreading them apart as I dart my tongue inside her, feeling the quick pulse of her muscles around me. I then slide my tongue back up her seam and suck on her hub of nerves there.

Stevie pulls my head back by my hair so that I'm forced to look up at her. She leans forward and whispers in my ear, "Are you ready to fuck me, Finn?"

I've found myself rolling my eyes in the past when a woman has tried to dirty talk me or be in charge. It often sounds forced or ridiculous, but not when it comes to Stevie. Not when she's pulling my hair and demanding that I fuck her. Not in the least.

I struggle to remember to unmute the phone. "Yes, I agree," I murmur to something Rowdy says, but my eyes are one hundred percent consumed with Stevie's.

I rise from my knees and capture my mouth over hers. I want her to taste how she tastes to me. I want her to see why I'm totally fucking consumed by that pussy of hers.

And by the time I'm done kissing her, I have my dick out of my zipper, am turning her around, and pushing her face down on my desk.

I take a moment to stare at her like that. Her ass, her thighs, her arousal glistening between them, and know I will never look at my desk the same again.

Ever.

I'll always picture her there with that *come-hither* look and her thighs spread for me.

I run a hand over the curve of her ass and then down between her slit, her body squirming beneath my touch.

"Finn?"

I turn mute off. "I'm listening, Rowd," I say as I slide the head of my cock up and down, wetting it with her wetness. She wiggles her ass against me and fucking hell, I do the only thing I can—give her what she wants.

I push my way into her, my eyes rolling back as she closes around me and takes me in as far as I'll go. I see stars. The pleasure owns every goddamn piece of me.

"Finn," she murmurs and her voice jolts me back to the here and now and that Rowdy's on the phone. I cover her mouth with my hand as I lick a line up her spine. The motion only serves to drive me deeper inside of her. At least my hand muffles her moan.

"Don't make a sound," I whisper into her ear. "Or I won't let you come."

Her laugh is deep and throaty and makes my balls tighter, if that's even possible. Being buried this deep has them tight already.

Jesus fucking Christ.

This woman.

She could drag me to the depths of hell, and I swear to God, I'd follow her.

I kiss my way back down her spine and begin to move. Slow, deep strokes that feel like every nerve ending in my cock is getting paid its due attention by her wet, tight heat.

The woman is definitely my drug. The feel of her. The taste of her. The sound of her.

I push my way in and grind hard against her as her hands reach out and grip the edge of the desk. Her teeth nip at my hand covering her mouth and—

"Sanderson. Am I talking to myself here?"

"My connection is breaking up," I say, trying to fight the breathlessness to my voice. "I'll have to call you back."

And without waiting for his response, I hang up the phone before sliding my hand from Stevie's mouth to fist in her hair.

"Thank God," she moans as I slam into her from behind, her body shoving against the desk and her skin moving with the connection. I do it again. And again.

"Harder," she groans.

I thrust as deep as I can go and get rewarded by how she tightens herself around me.

"Faster," she begs.

I lean over her, grinding into her again. "You'll get me, all right. Hard. Fast. Nonstop." I scrape my teeth over her shoulder. "But on my terms. In my way."

"Please." The breathlessness with which she says that single word is such a damn turn-on.

This time when I pick up the pace, there is no slowing down.

Not when she screams out my name and her body pulses all around me.

Not when my spine begins to tingle and my balls tighten as she milks me over the edge.

Not when it's her name on my lips this time.

My last thought as I find my release is *this* is going to hurt.

She is going to hurt.

Letting her go is going to hurt.

Chapter
FORTY-THREE

Stevie

"I'm on my way out," Faith says as she moves into the kitchen.

"Faith?" Finn asks looking over from where we sit on the couch. "It's past nine o'clock. I thought you left a long time ago."

"I know but I wanted to make sure you had everything you needed while I'm gone for a few days. The refrigerator in the garage has meals ready for you and—"

"Thank you," he says. "You didn't have to stay. Your family is probably missing you."

She snorts. "Stanley is too wrapped up in watching baseball tonight to even notice I'm gone." She waves her hand his way in dismissal and smiles.

"I doubt that."

"After thirty-five years, I know that when the Padres are on, he prefers me to be busy so I don't bug him."

"Well, have a great trip," Finn says.

"We will." I hear her keys rattle. "Oh, I forgot to ask. Did either of you drop this on your way in? It's brand new with the tag on it so I figured it's yours since it was just outside the gate by the mailbox."

Both Finn and I turn to look at what she's holding up, and I swear to God my breath stops at the sight of the red Nike ball cap in her hands.

Just like my dad used to wear.

It takes me a second to find both my feet beneath me and my words as I stand and move toward her. "Where did you . . ."

I take the hat from her, not thinking about it being someone else's despite the tag hanging from it and not really caring, because in an instant, I'm swamped with the grief that has been fading over time.

Tears well in my eyes as I stare at this hat. I can't help but think it's a sign from him. A something from the powers that be to tell me I'm doing okay and that he's still here with me.

"Thank you, Faith," Finn murmurs as he puts his arm around me and steers me to the couch before sitting on the table facing me. But I can't even bring myself to look up and meet his eyes because I'm so busy staring at this silly hat that somebody is missing.

"Tell me about him," Finn murmurs, his hands closing over mine as they hold on to the hat.

"He was my dad." I whisper the words and then realize that term doesn't have the same meaning for him that it does for me. "He was the only person I had for so long, that I don't know what life is like without him."

"I'm sure he felt the same way about you."

"He went to Mother's Day events and made a grand show of it so I wouldn't feel left out. I'm talking feather boas and glitter tiaras and he didn't give a rat's ass what people thought about him so long as I smiled. We'd celebrate Christmas in Australia, heading down early, before the Australian Open. He surprised me every year with the ugliest Christmas sweater I'd ever seen, and then we'd turn the air down in our hotel room to make it feel cold and wintery while we ate dinner and opened gifts. He signed cards pretending they were from my mother, even when he knew that I knew it was his handwriting. Birthdays were all-out events. He . . ." I hiccup over a sob as I remember the many ridiculous things he did that I've forgotten over time.

"He sounds amazing."

"Sometimes I think he tried too hard and did too much. It was part of the tension between us. He held on too tight when all I wanted to do was let go . . . but I wouldn't change it for the world."

Finn lifts one of my hands and kisses its palm. "He didn't tell you he was sick," he murmurs against my skin, and the pain of that hits me all over again.

My breath hitches as I nod, fighting back the tears. "I was so angry at him. Furious. You know?" I ask and Finn nods. "We fought for days over it, but then I became frantic because, how could I waste any time directing my anger at him when there wasn't much time left? As it was, he'd been suffering for over a year at that time."

I remember the loneliness the most. The feeling like I was adrift at sea with everyone trying to tether me and not a single one being successful at it.

Then came the guilt. The endless, debilitating guilt over being so wrapped up in myself and my world that I'd missed the signs. The weight he was losing that he said was due to a new vegan lifestyle. The exhaustion that was prevalent that he blamed on insomnia. His excuses I believed about why he was staying home here and there.

How could I not have noticed?

"I'm so sorry," Finn whispers and squeezes my hand.

I shrug to let the emotion burning in my throat subside. "His reasoning was that he didn't want me to stop living because of him." I sniff. "Up until the end, he was pouring his life into me so that I could have mine."

"Sounds like an incredible man."

I smile for the first time as I remember our last real conversation. "My last promise to him was that I'd win the US Open for him. It was his favorite tournament, and I was desperate to promise him anything to motivate him to keep fighting. To stay alive."

"That's understandable."

"So I promised him I'd win only if he was there in the stands. And then he died . . ."

"And you fought wanting to even train for the tournament because—"

"Because I was mad at him for not upholding his end of the bargain. And because I knew going there without him was going to reinforce his absence." I blow out a frustrated sigh. "I'd give anything to look in the stands one more time to see his red hat sitting there and hear him say those words to me."

"Game on, Stevester," Finn whispers.

The tears begin. They begin when I don't want them to. They continue when I realize it feels so damn good to let it all out. And they fall even harder until I'm all cried out and exhausted and then, Finn picks me up like I'm weightless and carries me to bed.

Chapter
FORTY-FOUR

Stevie

THE NIGHT BREEZE IS COOL AGAINST MY SKIN.

Finn's body is warm as I snuggle into him. My nose is under the curve of his jaw, and I find an odd comfort in the scrape of his stubble every time his chest rises and falls.

His arms tighten around me, his breath even in my ear, and I relish the relaxing sounds of the ocean muted through the closed slider door.

Here, I feel safe.

Here, I feel taken care of.

Here, I—

I startle awake, not ready for the dream to end just yet but when I do wake, I realize it isn't a dream this time.

This time I'm really lying in Finn's bed, *in his arms*, where now I remember he held me as I cried myself to sleep.

I broke down, broke apart, and he held me so the pieces that fell were able to be pieced back together when I was done.

My breath is shaky when I inhale because I'm petrified that I'm going to move, that he's going to wake up. And that when he does, he'll realize he brought me to his bed and freak out.

I press a kiss to his chest and close my eyes, trying to memorize the feel of his heart beating beneath my lips, the sound of him breathing, the scent of his skin . . . every single thing about him.

The tears fall again, this time silently, but for such very different reasons than before. This time it's because I've never let myself get so close to someone, to fall for someone, and now that I have, it's over.

I contemplate waking him up just so I can hear his voice and commit that sleepy rumble to memory too. But I know I'd be waking him up because every part of me wants to ask him to go with me.

To head to New York with me.

But he has a life he's put aside long enough for me.

It's time to let him live it.

Besides, the last thing he wants is to be with someone whose life is followed by cameras all the time and whose every move and business is reported somewhere, somehow.

So I feel sorry for myself and let the tears fall, as I breathe him in as long as I can.

Chapter
FORTY-FIVE

Stevie

"Honey, I'm home," I say as I walk into the house, well aware it's the last time I'm going to say it.

Even worse, there is no response. The usual banter from Finn isn't there.

I suddenly get emotional over its absence.

See? *What's sentimental to you doesn't even matter to him.*

But as soon as the thought passes through my mind, I see the box on the counter with a card on top that says "Open me, Stevie."

"What the . . ." I murmur as I tear open the card and then bark out a laugh when I read what's inside.

Cards O' Fun

Put this dress on and meet me upstairs in an hour.

My cheeks hurt from smiling so hard as I open the box to find a gorgeous, sparkly red dress along with a more than sexy pair of strappy heels.

Finn Sanderson, I don't know what you're doing for our last night, but I'm here for it.

At the hour mark, I glance in the mirror one more time before I leave my room to meet Finn.

The woman staring back at me is so very different than the one who was carried into this house two months ago. *She* was broken and beaten down. The woman looking back at me is confident, independent, and strong.

She's also putting on a brave face to try and enjoy whatever Finn has in store for her tonight instead of being sad about what comes tomorrow.

With a deep breath, I open my bedroom door and head upstairs where there is a patio on the roof.

I expect a romantic table for two with dinner and candlelight. That's the only thing my mind can come up with that Finn has done.

But when I clear the last step and look around, a little yelp escapes my mouth.

The rooftop patio is decked out like a high school prom. There's a photo booth, a deejay in the corner, sparkly decorations, and sashes for prom king and queen laid out on the table beside me.

And standing in the middle of it all is one Finn Sanderson with a tuxedo on, complete with a vest that matches my dress.

"Finn." It's all I can think to say as I take in all the special touches that are simply incredible.

"You said you never got to go to prom so I wanted to give you another first worth noting." He takes a step toward me, his grin captivating, and holds out a box for me.

"What's this?"

"No prom is complete without a corsage, right?"

I open the container and slip the corsage over my wrist. When I look up to meet his eyes, I have tears swimming in mine. "Thank you." I shake my head, at a loss for words. "No one has ever done anything this thoughtful for me before."

"Uh-uh." He lifts my chin up so I'm forced to meet his eyes. "Don't be sad. It's our prom night and you know what that means, right?"

"No." I giggle as the deejay starts up the music. Of course, it's one of the most popular songs of what would have been my prom year.

"It means it's time to party!" Finn yells.

And we do.

We dance like teenagers, drink spiked punch, and take way too many pictures in the photo booth. Photos I know I'll cherish in the weeks to come. We even have a mock crowning ceremony for the prom king and prom queen.

"What was your prom like?" I ask as we eat cupcakes by a firepit he set up overlooking the water.

"I'm pretty sure I drank too much. I know I didn't dance at all, except for the slow ones, because what eighteen-year-old guy doesn't not want to rub up against his date, and I know for certain we got home way past curfew because her dad was pissed."

"Why does that not surprise me?" I laugh.

He shrugs and laughs. "Because you know me too well." He leans forward and brushes his lips against mine.

"What was her name?" I ask.

"Who?"

"Your prom date."

"Jennifer Stevenson."

"Wow. No hesitation. I'm impressed." I laugh.

"Everyone remembers the name of who they went to prom with." He leans back and takes a sip of his beer.

I watch the ocean breeze flutter through his hair, and I take in the flames of the fire dancing in his eyes. We sit staring at this for some time, enjoying the moment, letting it soak in, and trying to commit it to memory to help us get through the coming days.

"Why?" I finally ask.

"Why what?"

"This." I hold my hands out to the elaborate setup and trouble he went through to do this for me.

"Because I wanted to. Because you deserve it. Because no one forgets their prom date."

And he doesn't want me to forget him.

Emotions burn in my throat at the unspoken words. The same ones swimming in his eyes as he takes my hand and leads me back to our private dance floor.

And as the night wears on to early morning, we slow dance to Maroon

5's "Daylight." We all but cling to each other as the song plays, trying to eek one last memory from the night.

And as we head downstairs, our hands linked and our hearts exhausted, Finn slowly undoes the zipper of my dress, lacing a row of kisses down my spine.

There is nothing hurried this time around. Nothing frantic like usual. It's soft kisses and tender touches. It's eye contact and hushed words.

There's grief and gratitude in our movements.

There's reverence and the need to remember.

There's a finality to it.

It's making love not just having sex.

And when Finn slips into me, when we come together as one, we start the process of saying goodbye.

Chapter
FORTY-SIX

Stevie

THE SUN IS BEGINNING TO LIGHTEN THE GRAY OF THE HORIZON through the sheer curtains in Finn's bedroom.

He lies tangled in the sheets, his body naked, and his soft snores filling the room.

I debated whether I should wake him up. Whether I would put ourselves through the finality of saying goodbye one more time.

But we already did that last night. In whispers of touch and hushed murmurs. In how we lay on the pillows staring at each other until he finally drifted off to sleep an hour ago, and I got up to pack.

I lean over and press a whisper of a kiss to his cheek. "Goodbye, Finn Sanderson," I murmur as I move toward the door.

But I look back one more time. It's too hard not to. And this time I hold my hand over my heart, pat three times, and smile at the man who holds my heart.

Because there's one more first worth noting as I leave this house: I'm in love with Finn Sanderson.

Chapter

FORTY-SEVEN

Finn

I WAKE WITH A START.

The sun is beaming through the windows but the house is absolutely silent. The bed beside me is cold to the touch.

I don't even call out for her because I already know by how the hint of her perfume still clings in the air.

She's gone.

Fucking gone.

Women always leave. Remember that.

"Fuck you, Dad," I mutter, my hands fisting in the comforter and my heart aching in my chest.

I expect bitterness to come. Anger. I anticipate the need to punch something . . . but there's nothing but a churning in my gut and a sudden emptiness in my heart.

She's gone. But she's gone because she's a tennis champion, and she's heading to work. To do what she's been working so hard for. *And that is perfectly okay*. It's what we knew was coming. It's what we've been preparing for. It's what she wants . . . and needs.

She didn't leave without cause. Is that the difference?

Did Dad ever find out why Mom left us? Why she could turn her back on her marriage and on her son?

I close my eyes and will myself back to sleep, thinking maybe it would be easier if I were bitter like my dad.

But I'm not.

This is something altogether different, and I don't know what the fuck to do about it.

I love you, Stevie.

I really do.

Chapter
FORTY-EIGHT

Finn

"How's she doing?" Faith asks with a lift of her chin to the television as she moves through the family room.

"She just won in straight sets." I glance her way but then go right back to the television. To where Stevie is sitting on her bench post-match, wiping the sweat off her face and then putting her rackets away.

"So that's good, right?"

"Yes." I smile distracted. "That's good."

I thought the ache in my chest would subside. It hasn't. I've thrown myself into my work the last few days but even that hasn't distracted me enough to forget.

Because how can you forget a woman like her?

Stevie stands and the camera follows her as she moves over to where Kellen stands with another man.

"You know you have a house in Manhattan, right?"

"What?" I ask Faith.

"The other place you live?"

"Yeah. What about it?"

"Isn't it only a few subway rides away from where she's playing right now?"

"Mm-hmm," I murmur as Stevie smiles and pats Kellen on the back.

I know the distance from my place. I've even looked up ticket availability and how to get there.

But sitting here, watching her in her element and doing her thing, I decide that my presence there would only be a distraction.

And if she's going to win this title, that's the last thing she needs.

This is what she does. She has a life of her own that has nothing to do with mine and . . .

Stevie looks toward where the camera is, and I swear to God, it feels like she's looking straight at me.

It would be an impossible stretch. With me normally in New York and her in Florida. For us to try and make it work. It would—

It was a good run.

I'll leave it at that.

But that doesn't make it any easier when I stand in my kitchen later that night and look at the door waiting for her to come in and ask how my day was.

Chapter
FORTY-NINE

Stevie

Did he watch today? Did he see me advance to the quarterfinals?

Did he see me hand over my heart when I patted it three times before the match started?

Does he know how much I'd kill to look up and see him sitting in the stands?

Or waiting in the locker room afterward where he'd be pacing while on his phone, talking too loud, sucking up all the air, and dominating the space?

I look at my phone, scrolling past texts from Carson and Vivi and Jordan, and hate that the one person I most want one from isn't there.

For all I know, he could be on a plane somewhere right now. Or anywhere really. Just not here.

With a deep breath, I prepare myself for my post-game interviews.

But not before one more look down at my phone.

Nothing.

Does he know how much I miss him?

Chapter FIFTY

Finn

"Hasn't this gone on long enough?"

I smile when I hear Chase Kincade's voice coming through my phone. "Hasn't what gone on long enough? You hating me?" I ask playfully, knowing we're way past that.

"I don't hate you and you know that."

"But you did."

"You're damn right I did, and I had valid reasons to after what you did to me—"

"True."

"But that's over and done with. I've moved on."

"How is Gunner, by the way?" I ask of her new husband who, by all accounts, seems like a nice guy and makes her ridiculously happy.

"Wonderful." I can hear the smile in her voice. "You're distracting me, Sanderson."

"Yes. I forgot. What's gone on long enough?"

"This whole stealing clients back and forth bullshit."

"You're upset about Dante," I say, proud that I was able to pull him on board with my firm.

"I'm upset about a lot of people."

"As am I," I counter. "I think we're pretty even in the stealing clients department." It's been an exhausting few years trying to hold on to what is mine while staunching off an all-out attack from her firm to try and steal my clients away.

I may have deserved it. That much I can admit.

"Then I say we call a truce."

I chuckle and give a shrug she can't see. "Okay."

"Okay?" Surprise rings through her tone. "Are you feeling okay? You never just *okay* anything, especially when it comes to giving up potential income."

"I said okay. Can we leave it at that?"

Chase falls silent for a beat before making a noncommittal sound. "Who is she?"

"Who is who?" I play dumb.

"Something is different in your life when you're a man who never likes change so the one thing that has to be different is that you found someone."

"That's quite the stretch, Chase, even for you."

"And you forget that I *know you*, Finn Sanderson."

My silence is enough of an answer but instead of rubbing my nose in it, Chase stays silent too.

I struggle with an answer. Telling her, not telling her.

"I found her and let her go," I finally say and fuck does it feel good to just say it to someone.

"Why would you do something stupid like that?"

My chuckle is self-deprecating. "Because . . . fuck if I know, Chase."

"You just let her walk away?"

"You know me . . . you know my dad—that I can't undo years of fear—"

"If you like her as much as this conversation is implying, then you'll figure your shit out and figure it out real quick."

"She scares the shit out of me."

Her laugh fills my ears. "You're damn right she does. Love does that to you. It scares the shit out of you. It makes you fear having the person as much as not having the person. It owns your heart and head until it's all you can think about."

Her words are a poignant nail on the head that reinforce how I feel.

"I'll think about it."

"Go get the girl, Finn. If there is one thing I've learned from Gunner, it's that life doesn't hold any guarantees. We don't always get second chances, Finn. But I think you're getting yours. Ignore the shit your dad told you. Follow your heart. You know that we Kincade girls didn't believe in love either, and yet here we are, all blissfully happy. And now it's your turn. Geography doesn't matter, Finn. When you love someone, you're willing to make sacrifices that benefit them. And it looks like that's what you need to do."

Is that what I need to do? *Give up my excuses, my bachelor ways?* But what the fuck am I really giving up? *When you love someone, you're willing to make sacrifices that benefit them.*

"Oh, and congrats on that interview a few months back. The Stevie Lancaster one. That was brilliant agenting 101."

"Did you just give me a compliment?" I tease, relieved to be on more neutral territory than talking about my current love life with an ex.

"I'll plead the fifth if you ever tell anyone."

"Funny."

"The Open is over in a week. You need to get your ass in gear if you're going to win her back."

"How did you—"

"The whole world saw it in that photo with the Greshenko match. I'm just glad to hear this time the picture that told a thousand words was true."

Chapter
FIFTY-ONE

Stevie

Finn: Congrats on making it to the semifinals. It was a great match.

I stare at the text, my pulse pounding, and my smile widening.

Me: Thank you. How are you?

Finn: Good. Busy. Just working. You look great out there.

A million responses fly through my mind. *I miss you. I love you. I want to see you.* But I type none of them because as much as I want to get my hopes up, I can't. This is a simple text after a week of not talking to him, not a declaration of love.

Me: Thank you. Off to the press circus now. Thanks for texting.

My sigh is audible as I stare at his words, missing him terribly.

FIFTY-TWO

Finn

"Okay. So read that paragraph again. I need you to understand the parameters of this endorsement deal," I say to Moni, a WNBA star, as I click on the television in my office. "I'll wait while you do."

Stevie's semifinals match coverage should be starting any moment, and I don't want to miss it.

I take a seat and go to square up some loose-leaf papers on my desk when Stevie comes onto the screen. She's warming up, hitting a few balls over the net. Right before the camera pans off her, she looks at it, puts her hand over her heart, and taps three times.

I grab my remote and rewind the broadcast, needing to see it again. *Did she . . . was that for me?*

If so, I need to make sure she's telling me what I want to hear. See. That she feels the same way about me that I do her.

You showed him that hearts matter. That knowing someone loves you matters.

And it's there. Plain as day. The three taps.

She wants me to know that she loves me, and that I matter to her. I stand up. I sit down. I rewind it to see it again as adrenaline races through my veins.

She fucking loves me.

But how do I show her the same thing? How do I make sure she knows that her heart matters too?

Chapter
FIFTY-THREE

Stevie

WHEN I COLLAPSE ONTO THE MASSAGE TABLE, MY BODY IS EXHAUSTED and my morale is for shit.

"I don't know what the big deal is. You had a bad match. You still won, so let's watch the tapes, see what we can fix, and be ready for the finals."

I close my eyes and ignore Kellen. I know he means well—it seems everyone does these days—but he's also never been my coach when I've done poorly. He doesn't realize that I don't need to be coddled—Christ, do I not need to be coddled—but rather I need to be told that yes, I did play like shit.

"Go away, Kell," I mumble, needing space and time to be grumpy.

My form sucked. I was late going to the right when the ball was hit there. My serve was off. Yes, I won, but there is no way in hell I'm going to beat Martina Hauerr in the finals playing like this.

It's my father's voice I'm missing right now. His strong but valid criticisms. His unwanted critiques. His scant praise that made me want to work hard in order to get more of it.

I lie face down and wait for Angel, the masseuse, to ease the tension and soreness in my muscles before I jump into the ice bath.

But it's only then with my face in the weird hole thing on the massage table that I shut my eyes and allow myself to come down from the high from winning . . . *and* the pressure from not performing up to par.

It's then that the tears well and fall onto the floor beneath me.

He should be here. My father. He should be in the chair opposite me telling me what I need to work on before the next match. I should hear his baritone laugh as he scrolls through social media and reads the ridiculous comments about the match. I should feel his kiss on the back of my head and his soft words, "I'm proud of you," before he leaves the room to go review the tapes before me.

Dad, I need you here with me. It's hard. Everything is so different without you here sitting in those seats, your presence willing me to win. I miss you so much.

I miss him. But I also need to win for him. After all the years of sacrifice, of time, of direction, of praise, of coaching . . . of loving me. This win needs to be for him. I'll regret it if I don't get my butt into gear and win the US Open for my dad.

And yet, that also makes me see what else I regret.

I should have told Finn that I love him. That this could work somehow.

I miss Finn too.

I sniff the tears away as Angel walks into the room with her cheerful greeting and heaven-sent hands.

After the Open.

I need to do what I came here to do first.

Win my dad's favorite tournament. For the first man in the world I loved. *To honor him.*

Chapter
FIFTY-FOUR

Stevie

THE LOCKER ROOM IS SILENT.

Silent except for the noise in my head that won't shut up. The little tweaks I need to make. Martina's game plan in how she approaches matches. But I welcome the noise because it's so much better than the quiet I've been struggling with these past few days.

"There is a text I think you need to see," Kellen says, interrupting my thoughts as I watch Hayley hand him my phone.

I'm about to snap at him because he knows better than to pull me out of my preparation-for-match mode, but the look on his face stops me.

"You need to see this," he says as I take my phone from him.

My heart flips in my chest when I see that it's from Finn. Even more when I read the words.

Finn: I thought this might help you today.

And when I push play on the video, the tears just come. One after another after another until they hit my smiling lips. It's a video montage of my dad saying, "Game on, Stevester." It looks like it's every time the television cameras captured Dad, from when I was around twelve, on a high school sports channel, up until my last game with him in my box.

He has his beloved red hat on, and I get to hear his voice over and over in his distinctly raspy voice there.

When it ends, I watch it again. This time the tears dry sooner and my smile grows a little bit wider.

He brought him to me. Finn gave me my dad in the final match of the tournament I promised him I'd win.

My hands are shaking as I try to type.

Me: Thank you. This means the world to me.

I hit send, holding tight to the phone as if it were his hand.

Finn: Just like you mean to me.

I stare at his text, my hope bubbling up in a way I never thought it could. In a way that has my breath catching and my heart racing.

Me: Meaning?

"Meaning I've been missing you like crazy, and I think we need to figure out how to not make me miss you."

I stare at my phone, so very afraid to look up and hope that it's him, here in the flesh, even though I know it is.

There are footsteps—as Kellen's and Hayley's leave the room and as Finn's come into view in front of me.

"Important firsts are supposed to be noted so let's take note of this one." Finn's fingers find my chin and lift it up so that I'm forced to look into those gorgeous eyes of his. And what I see in them is exactly how I feel reflected back at me. "I'm in love with you, Stevie Lancaster. Ridiculously in love with you when I'm not a man who believes in love at all."

I rise to my feet as if I'm on autopilot. My body and heart already reacting before my mind can process his words.

"So tell me you're in love with me too. Tell me the past two weeks have been as miserable without me as they've been for me without you. Even though you have played like the incredibly talented tennis champion you are. Tell me that we'll figure out how to make this work because damn it, woman, you're *my* Cards O' Fun, and I want to keep turning them over and experiencing each different one with you. Only you."

Tears slip down my cheeks as I struggle to find words to respond. As I try to figure out how to make him understand what I'm feeling inside. And there's a moment between our eyes meeting and our lips meeting where the world stops for a few seconds, and the only thing I can think of, anticipate, dream of, is his kiss. A moment so poignant and perfect that when I brush my lips against his and breathe him in, I know this is the beginning.

This is my future. He is my forever.

"I love you too," I murmur. He wraps his arms around me and holds me tight, causing me to feel completed and complemented in a way I never have before.

"Now, tell me exactly what you know about Martina Hauerr's game and how to beat her. Because this is your win, Lancaster. Prove to me that you're ready to take that crown. Show me what it takes. Get out there and win. Let's go."

And that's what I needed to hear. That gruff, authoritarian, no-bull-shit encouragement.

Victory, here I come.

Chapter
FIFTY-FIVE

Finn

FOR A MAN WHO WAS TAUGHT TO SHUN LOVE, TO SHUN EMOTION, it's impossible to put into words what it's like watching the woman you love—yes, love—get ready to battle on the court with the world watching.

There's color in her cheeks and a smile on her lips. There's a swagger in her step and confidence in her attitude that I love knowing I helped put there.

She completes her warm-up and steps over to the bench to wipe the sweat from her brow.

My chest feels like it's going to burst with a pride I don't think I've ever experienced before. For her, battling to be in this moment after everything she went through, and for me, finally putting to rest my dad's rhetoric that he spent a lifetime trying to make me believe.

Not all women leave.

Some battle. Perhaps even fall. But if you hold out your hand long enough, be patient enough, and make yourself just as vulnerable as they feel, then you just might change the cycle.

"Quiet, please," the chair umpire says to the stadium, as both Stevie and Martina walk to their respective ends of the court.

I've played this over in my head on the flight. Just how I'll do this. So that Stevie will be reminded of her father while at the same time starting something that is uniquely ours. This won't be the last time I'm sitting courtside, cheering her on.

I slip the red Nike hat onto my head.

Hell, might as well take note of this important first too.

"Game on, Rapunzel."

Epilogue

Stevie

FINN GROANS BESIDE ME AT THE BRIGHT SUNLIGHT GLARING THROUGH the windows of our rental house. "It's winter. Doesn't Australia know that?" he says as he rolls onto his back and sighs loudly. We've both been having trouble adjusting to the time difference, but that's why we're here so early. To get acclimated before the Australian Open starts so it doesn't affect me when I play.

And so we can have some added bonus time together.

"But it's summer here. The sun and heat are a welcome change from the cold of New York." I shift, sliding my arm beneath the pillow my head is propped on so I can study him. His dark hair. His profile. The rise and fall of his bare chest. The pillow creases on his cheek.

I love him.

It's plain and simple. I love him in a way I never knew was possible. But I feel like we're going through a rough patch. Between training for the Australian Open and his work taking him all over the place, I feel like we're never on the same page.

That's why I'm so very grateful he's here with me. And I'm hoping that this added extra downtime together in Melbourne will help with that.

"You're staring at me," he murmurs but keeps his face aimed at the ceiling.

"I am."

"Humph."

"What's that supposed to mean?"

"Nothing. It's just a sound." He sighs and turns on his side so that we're face to face. Butterflies take flight in my stomach even after being with him for almost eighteen months.

Yes, I count.

Every day is another I get with him. Each month something I'm grateful for.

Our eyes meet and there's something in his. Something I can't decipher.

"Now, you're staring at me," I whisper and reach out to put my hand on his heart and tap three times. His smile is as soft as his sigh. "Are you okay?"

"Mm-hmm."

"*Mm-hmm?* Can we do better than that?" I ask. He's been off. And off not in the sense that he's Finn and he's always doing a hundred things, but *off* in the fact that he's been distant, and I don't know how to reel him back in.

A flash of a smile. His hand reaching out to tuck a strand of hair behind my ear. A glimpse of the old Finn.

"I've been busy negotiating a contract," he says. "It's been a tough one to figure out all the angles and caveats. I'm not certain my client will accept it."

I startle. I had no idea he had something big going on. And then I breathe a sigh of relief because that means this distance I've felt is not because something is wrong with us, but rather he's just stressed over work.

I exhale a soft sigh of relief. "Want to talk about it?"

He shrugs, his fingers tracing up and down the length of my arm. "It's a lifetime contract that—"

"Wow!" Now I definitely want to ask who it is, but we agreed a long time ago that I can't ask specifics when it comes to his clients and their negotiations.

"I know. So it's a big deal that I make sure all the terms are right."

"I'm assuming it's an endorsement deal?" Nike or the like as a lifetime deal is few and far between, but Finn has clients who are worthy of them.

"More like a partnership of sorts."

"Okay." I draw the word out. "That's even rarer."

"I know, so you can see why I've been stressing over it."

"I would be too. No wonder you've been lost in thought more times than not."

He gives me that half-smile again that melts my heart. "I'm sorry." He brings my hand up to his lips and presses a kiss to my palm. "I didn't mean to be preoccupied or ignore you." That half-smile lights up the room in the best way possible. "Forgive me?"

"Of course. Always." *Forever.* "What is troubling you?"

"The terms."

"What about them?"

"I want to get them right. How the two parties deal when one of them is unhappy since that is bound to happen."

"Naturally."

"Or what happens if she—"

"*She?*" I ask, surprised by his slip, when he's normally so guarded.

He scrunches his nose in the most adorable way. "Yes, *she.*"

"What else?"

"I don't know. I mean, what if I work this hard on something and she rejects the offer? What if she's not willing to sign a lifetime contract? What if she thinks I'll fall short in taking care of her? What if—"

"What if the sky falls and the world stops turning?" I tease as I reach out and squeeze his hand. This is so not like Finn. He's always so secure, so confident. "I'm sure she trusts you and your advice and all you bring to the table, because hasn't she already agreed to be with you in some way or another?"

His smile softens. "True."

I lean forward and press a kiss to his lips. "Don't move, I have something for you." I scoot off the bed and head to the other room to grab the two boxes I've hidden in the coat closet that most definitely isn't being used in this heat. Maybe this will lighten the mood and make him smile.

When I walk back in, I'm struck by the sight of him. Finn is sitting up against the headboard, pillows propped behind him with his tanned skin so very striking against the white sheets.

"What's this?"

"Just a little Christmas present for you."

"For me? But Christmas isn't for two days."

I take a seat before him, sitting cross-legged on the bed, and feel a little punch of desire as his eyes dart down to where the hem of my T-shirt has crept up to show my nakedness beneath.

"I know, but I think it's time we continue a tradition in our own way."

He narrows his brows. "Now I'm definitely curious." He takes the box from me and opens the card on top. His eyes light up when he chuckles at the card I tried to replicate from the one he has in a frame on his desk. "We're playing Cards O' Fun now, are we?"

"Perhaps."

He toys with the card's edges before pulling it from the envelope. His laugh reverberates around the room and fills me with love. "Take me somewhere in public and wear this," he reads. "That's not much of a dare."

I motion for him to open it. His eyes are locked on mine as he pulls the ribbon off ever so slowly. "You never know. It could be some lacey lingerie or—"

"Ha. You wouldn't, because you know I'd be photographed with you."

He has a point. But it's his laugh when he sees what's inside that makes me smile. He pulls out a multicolor ugly Christmas sweater that has Flynn Rider, also known as Rapunzel's prince, on it.

He shakes his head and chuckles as he slides it over his head and stares at me while I pull out my Rapunzel one and slip it over my head.

"These look like Disney threw up all over us," he says.

"I know. *They're perfect.*"

"I have other words I think I could use but we'll stick with yours." He angles his head to the side and leans forward. "Thank you. It's my favorite, just like you are." He presses a kiss to my lips that warms my insides.

"So you'll wear it to take me out to breakfast?"

"That's not much of a dare, Lancaster."

His tongue slips between my lips, and I fall into his kiss. His taste. The sounds he makes. Does this ever get old? Will it?

For some reason, I just don't think it will.

"Maybe breakfast can wait," I say, shifting so that I'm straddling him, our bodies fitting together perfectly.

"It can, can't it?" His lips touch mine as his hands slide up and hold my hips.

"It can."

"What about my present for you?" he asks.

"I think you're about to give it to me." I laugh as I grind where his cock is pressed against his underwear.

"True," he laughs, but he then brings his hands up to frame my face and tilts my head back so he can meet my eyes. There's an intensity to the emotions swimming in his eyes. A clarity that I haven't seen before.

"What?" I ask softly.

"I have something for you," he says and then clears his throat. "And I've been stressing over how to give it to you and what to say and how we can negotiate the terms to your liking—"

"The terms?" I purse my lips. "Are you telling me that the lifetime contract you were negotiating was for me?"

"Not *for you*, but more like *with you*."

"Finn, what are you talking about?" I laugh and then it falls off when Finn pulls a black velvet box out from beneath the pillow beside him. "*Oh.*"

His smile is tentative. "I've been worried about all the ways I could convince you that this would be a good deal for you. So that you might look at this and see something other than how much I benefit by you taking this deal. But no matter how much I tried, all I can think about is how much both of us entered into this wanting nothing, and how we ended up finding *everything*."

"Finn." My voice wavers as I say his name and realize the contract he's been negotiating isn't with Nike or a sports company. *It's between him and me.*

So like my Finn. The one I'm staring at right now through tear-blurred eyes and with a heart that's all but swelling out of my chest. My Finn, who has to dot every I and cross every T. My Finn, who is always looking out for those who have put their trust in him to do the best for them.

"So I can't promise you that I'll always be the best partner in this deal. I can't promise that you won't feel taken for granted or that I won't ask too much of you . . . but I can promise you whatever hard times we face, we can always meet at the bargaining table to work it out. And what I can tell you is that *I love you, Stevie Lancaster*. I love that you take chances. That you're dedicated and spontaneous and that you love with all your heart, even when you don't realize you're doing it. And most of all, I love that you love me. A man who might be hard to love, but who would move heaven and earth to hear your laugh. To taste your kiss. To lie beside you each and every night."

My pulse races and my hands shake. Tears well in his eyes before he looks at the box in his hand and then looks back up at me.

"So I promise to celebrate your victories and be the person you lean against after your defeats. More than anything, I promise to take note of every incredible first with you. Will you marry me?"

When he opens the box, a little laugh escapes when I see in the top of the ring box, he has his own homemade Cards O' Fun that says, "Say yes."

And then I gasp at the delicate band framing a princess cut diamond. It's gorgeous but the man who's holding it outshines its beauty by miles.

When I meet his eyes, I know he was built to love me. Every complicated inch of me. And I also know from spending the last eighteen months with him, that this is a man my dad would have loved *for* me too.

"Yes," I whisper. "More than yes. Yes, times a trillion."

And before he can even put the ring on my finger, I launch myself at him, my lips on his, my body against his, and show him just how beneficial this lifetime contract will be.

Have you fallen in love . . .

Have you fallen in love with the whole Play Hard series?

Hunter and Dekker took their sweet time finding love in
Hard to Handle.

Then Rush swept you off your feet in his and Lennox's
story *Hard to Hold*.

Not to be overshadowed was Drew and Brexton in *Hard to Score*.

And then there was the unexpected in Chase and Gunner's story in
Hard to Lose.

I hope you enjoy them!

About the Author

New York Times Bestselling author K. Bromberg writes contemporary romance novels that contain a mixture of sweet, emotional, a whole lot of sexy, and a little bit of real. She likes to write strong heroines and damaged heroes who we love to hate but can't help to love.

A mom of three, she plots her novels in between school runs and soccer practices, more often than not with her laptop in tow and her mind scattered in too many different directions.

Since publishing her first book on a whim in 2013, Kristy has sold over one and a half million copies of her books across twenty different countries and has landed on the *New York Times, USA Today,* and *Wall Street Journal* Bestsellers lists over thirty times. Her Driven trilogy (*Driven, Fueled, and Crashed*) is currently being adapted for film by the streaming platform, Passionflix.

With her imagination always in overdrive, she is currently scheming, plotting, and swooning over her latest hero. You can find out more about him or chat with Kristy on any of her social media accounts. The easiest way to stay up to date on new releases and upcoming novels is to sign up for her newsletter or follow her on Bookbub.

Made in the USA
Columbia, SC
27 May 2022

60960700R10137